The Glow They Left Behind

Mariz Everly

Copyright © 2025 Mariz Everly

All rights reserved

Published by: Moonlit Ever

Cover design by: Anze Ban Virant- ABV atelier Design

The characters and events portrayed in this book are fictitious. Any similarity to real persons, living or dead, is coincidental and not intended by the author.

For the patient who told me that I mattered —your words echoed loud in 2020 and carried me through...

PREFACE

When I began writing *The Glow They Left Behind*, I didn't fully grasp the weight of what this story would become—not just for the characters, but for myself. Nursing has always been more than a career for me; it's a calling that stretches far beyond hospital walls. It's about bearing witness to the most intimate and vulnerable moments in people's lives: their triumphs, their struggles, their fears, and, sometimes, their final breath.

In those moments, I've often wondered about the traces we leave behind. Is it the words we spoke, the dreams we didn't finish, or the love we shared? Perhaps it's the glow of our presence, faint but enduring, that lingers with those we touched—something that refuses to be extinguished, even when we're gone.

This book reflects the quiet yet profound ways we hold on to what matters most.

Lila's journey in *The Glow They Left Behind* mirrors my own in many ways. Her struggle to understand her gift, her calling, resonates deeply with my experiences as a nurse. Like her, I've faced moments of uncertainty and fear, moments where the line between holding on and letting go blurred beyond recognition.

This story is for anyone who has ever felt the pull of something greater than themselves, who has wondered about the lives they've intersected with, and who has sought meaning in the quiet glimmers of humanity. It's for the patients who taught me more than any textbook ever could, the ones who left their glow behind for me to carry forward.

Thank you for stepping into this world with me. I hope you find it haunting, moving, and, most of all, a reminder that even in the stillness of absence, there is a light that endures.

PROLOGUE

Hospitals carry echoes. Not the kind you hear in the hallways or the soft hum of machines, but echoes of lives lived and lost, of joy and despair tangled in a single breath. I used to think I knew what it meant to work in a place like this—long shifts, endless coffee, and the steady rhythm of saving lives.

At first, I chalked it up to exhaustion. Night shifts could play tricks on anyone. But then I started seeing them—the shadows that didn't belong, the eyes that lingered too long, faces I couldn't recognize but somehow knew.

The dead don't rest as easily as we'd like to believe. Some drift quietly into whatever comes next. Others linger, tethered to something they can't leave behind. And me? I became their keeper.

It's strange how quickly you adapt. One moment, I was an overworked nurse just trying to get through another shift. The next, I was a bridge between two worlds—patching up the living while trying to understand the dead. I didn't ask for this gift. I didn't even want it.

There was a glow to them, the ones who stayed. Not a literal light, but something deeper; fragments of who they were, who they wanted to be, and the things they couldn't let go of. Sometimes, it was heartbreakingly simple—a toy, a letter, a promise. Other times, it was darker, heavier, the kind of weight that bends a soul until it can't move forward.

Nightfall Pines wasn't supposed to be like this. I came here to escape, to find quiet after the chaos of the city. Instead, I found whispers in the dark and shadows that stretched too far.

They take pieces of us with them, and in turn, they leave their own behind. A glow, a mark, a memory.

I used to think death was the end. Now I know better. It's not an end; it's a threshold. And some thresholds take more than courage to cross.

CHAPTER ONE: FRESH START

The road stretched endlessly before me. The pine trees seemed to lean closer with every passing mile. The fog swallowed the horizon, leaving only my old sedan's headlights to light the way. Each mile brought with it a growing sense of hope. I drove through the roads by the Oregon coast I once would have called this scenery serene, a perfect backdrop for a fresh start—and now, that's exactly what it was.

I gripped the wheel tighter, my heart lighter than it had been in months. After everything I'd been through, this felt like a chance to breathe again, to rediscover who I was. The chaos of the hospital trauma center I used to work was behind me now, somewhere on the crowded streets of Los

Angeles. I could find peace here in the quiet expanse of Nightfall Pines.

When I finally saw the wooden sign that read "Welcome to Nightfall Pines," I exhaled shaky. The sign was old, its paint chipped and faded, giving it a charm that felt almost magical. The words felt like a promise rather than a greeting. This was the sanctuary I'd been searching for.

The town emerged from the fog, a collection of weathered buildings lining cobblestone streets. The streetlights cast a soft, warm glow, illuminating quaint storefronts and cozy homes. It was the opposite of everything I'd known—calm, quiet, and untouched by the rush of modern life. For the first time in a long while, I felt like I could exhale without the weight of the world pressing down on me.

Nightfall Pines Regional Hospital came into view as I drove up a slight incline. Perched on a hill, the two-story brick building stood tall and steady, its ivy-covered facade blending perfectly with the surrounding pines. The sight made me slightly shiver, but not from fear—it felt like destiny. It was where I was meant to be.

I parked in the nearly empty lot, the gravel crunching beneath my tires. As I stepped out, the scent of pine and salt air hit me, mingling with the faint smell of rain. I pulled my coat tighter and grabbed my bag. The air was crisp and alive, a far cry from the smog-filled haze of the city. I couldn't have imagined a better place to start over.

"You can do this," I whispered to myself, the words coming easily now. My voice carried a sense of determination, as though saying it out loud would make it true. This was my chance to heal, to make a difference again—not just for others, but for myself.

The hospital's doors creaked as I pushed them open. I got here just perfectly in time, after the shift change, just past 8 pm. Inside, the lobby was warmly lit with the soft murmurs of distant conversations. A reception desk stood to the right, cluttered with papers and an old computer. It had the kind of lived-in feel that immediately put me at ease.

"Lila?" a voice called, startling me. I turned to see a man in his early forties approaching. His scrubs were slightly wrinkled, and his ID badge dangled from his shirt pocket.

"That's me," I said, adjusting my bag on my shoulder.

"I'm Luis Mercado," he said with a friendly grin, extending his hand. "One of the ER nurses. Welcome to Nightfall Pines Regional. Let me grab someone from the desk to get you sorted."

As Luis walked off, I felt a presence behind me. Quickly turning, I caught a glimpse of a woman in a nurse's uniform near the far hallway. Her name tag glinted in the light; I could only make out the word Nurse Supervisor. She didn't look my way, and before I could call out, she disappeared around the corner. She looked intimidating, but I shook off the feeling, telling myself I'd meet her soon enough.

Luis returned with a clipboard and a stack of papers. "Paperwork first and badge picture," he said with mock seriousness. "But don't worry. It's not too bad."

As I filled out the forms, Luis leaned against the counter, chatting casually about the hospital and the town. "You'll like it here," he said. "Small team, but we're like family. And it's quiet... most of the time."

"That sounds perfect," I replied. "It's exactly what I needed."

After the paperwork, Luis led me to the nurses' station, introducing me to a few staff members along the way. Their smiles were warm and welcoming, and I felt a sense of hope that this place could truly be home.

"Luis, we've got incoming!" a voice called from down the hall. Another nurse leaned out from a doorway; her expression hurried but not panicked.

"Duty calls," Luis said with a smile. "You'll be fine here. I'll catch up with you later."

I nodded and thanked him as he disappeared down the hall. Left alone, I took a moment to take in the station. It felt oddly familiar, like a distant echo of my past experiences in the trauma center, but without the chaos and tension. Instead, there was a strange calm here, like the building itself was taking a deep breath.

I wandered a little further down the hallway, my curiosity getting the better of me. A set of double doors marked "Restricted" caught my attention. The paint on the doors was slightly darker than the rest of the hallway, and the brass handles looked worn from years of use. I hesitated for a moment before stepping closer.

"Can I help you?" a voice asked from behind me, making me jump. I turned to see a woman with a warm smile, her eyes kind but tired. She wore scrubs, and her name tag read "Maggie Kane- RT."

"Just getting my bearings," I said quickly. "I'm new here."

"Welcome aboard," Maggie said. "That wing's been closed off for years. There's not much to see there but dust and old equipment. I'm Maggie, Respiratory therapist"

I nodded, letting her words settle over me. Still, I couldn't shake the feeling that there was more to those doors than met the eye. Maggie's presence, though, was grounding. "Thanks," I said. "I'm Lila."

"Nice to meet you, Lila. When do you start?"

"I start the day after tomorrow, night shift," I said.

"We have a pretty good night shift team here. If you need anything, just holler. We're all pretty laid back around here." Maggie assured.

After Maggie left, I allowed myself another glance at the doors. They felt like a threshold to a secret that the hospital quietly held, something tethered to its history.

I could feel a faint, unexplainable pull, but I turned away and headed back to the station.

My first shift hadn't even started yet, but the mix of comfort and curiosity was growing.

By the time I returned to my car, the fog outside had thickened, swirling around the streetlights like ghostly tendrils. I glanced back at the hospital, its windows glowing softly in the night. A faint movement at one of the windows caught my eye, but when I looked closer, it was empty.

Shaking my head, I climbed into my car. "Just nerves," I muttered to myself. "That's all this is."

The drive to my rented cottage was short, the winding road barely visible in the dense fog. The small house perfectly reflected the quaint, modest, and quiet town. It's by the woods. Inside, I set my bag down and sank onto the sofa. It had been a long day, and though my body ached with exhaustion, my mind buzzed with the possibilities of this new life.

As I lay in bed that night, staring at the faint shadows dancing on the ceiling, I couldn't shake the feeling that Nightfall Pines held something extraordinary. It wasn't just a town—it was a puzzle, and I was about to become a piece of it. With that thought, I drifted into a restless sleep, my dreams filled with the faces I had yet to meet and the secrets I had yet to uncover.

CHAPTER TWO: NIGHTFALL PINES

As I drove through the dense forest of Nightfall Pines, the heart of the town unfolded before me. It was picturesque in an almost timeless way, as though it had been plucked from an old postcard.

Small houses with tidy gardens lined the streets, their porches adorned with seasonal decorations. A man waved to a woman carrying a basket of apples across the road, and she called back a friendly greeting. It was the kind of place where everyone seemed to know each other, where a wave wasn't just polite but expected.

I slowed as I passed the town's centerpiece: a white-steepled church surrounded by a wrought-iron fence. Directly across from it was the town cemetery, its headstones weathered and each one a silent story waiting to be uncovered. A couple of people stood by a grave, their heads bowed in quiet reflection, adding to the peaceful yet solemn air.

The fire station was only a couple of blocks from the church, its red doors open and revealing a gleaming fire truck. A firefighter leaned against the engine, chatting with someone who appeared to be dropping off baked goods. It made me smile.

Further down, I spotted a small Thai restaurant tucked into the corner with a hand-painted sign, "Thai Tasty," which was slightly faded but still vibrant. A "Since 1985" plaque hung proudly beside the door. Clearly, this place was a cornerstone of the community, one that had stood the test of time.

My stomach growled, but I resisted the urge to stop because I wanted to finish my errands. I turned onto the main street, where the shops were next to each other, Each storefront was unique, from the general store with its bright awning to a boutique with handmade clothes displayed in the window. The Warm Nook coffee shop caught my eye as I passed it. Its large windows revealed warm lighting and shelves filled with books, promising a respite I would need later.

The grocery store was just ahead, its small parking lot already half-full. I pulled in and parked, taking a moment to soak in the view. Nightfall Pines wasn't just charming—it was alive in a way I hadn't felt in years. There was a quiet energy here, a community and history that I couldn't quite explain.

The air was crisp and cool as I stepped out of my car, the morning fog still clinging. Nightfall Pines was slowly coming to life, with shopkeepers flipping their signs to "Open" and the light conversation drifting from the bakery on the corner. It was my first full day in town, and I was determined to explore, starting with the grocery shopping.

I adjusted my scarf against the chill and made my way down the narrow sidewalk, passing the small buildings. Each one seemed to have a story, with their weathered shutters and cheerful aura. It was the kind of town where time slowed down, inviting you to enjoy every detail

The grocery store, called "Pines Market," It's nestled between a hardware store and a gift shop selling handmade trinkets. Its sign is painted in faded blue-green letters. It was swaying from the breeze. The smell of freshly baked bread greeted me as I pushed the door open, and I couldn't help but smile at the familiar comfort of it.

Inside, the aisles were narrow and packed with an eclectic mix of goods. Something was charming about how the shelves were stocked—not with the clinical precision of a big chain store, but with the care of someone who genuinely wanted to provide for their neighbors.

As I browsed, adding items to my basket, I felt eyes on me. It was subtle but unmistakable. Small-town curiosity, I thought. When I reached the checkout counter, the cashier—a woman in her late forties with salt-and-pepper hair tied into a loose bun—greeted me with a warm smile.

"Good morning," she said, scanning my items. Her name tag read "Candice." "You must be the new nurse at Nightfall Pines Hospital from California."

I blinked, caught off guard by how quickly the town's grapevine worked. "I am," I admitted with a small laugh.

Candice's eyes twinkled with interest. "Well, welcome to Nightfall Pines. I'm Candice. Everyone's been talking about you since they heard we were getting a nurse. Must've been a big change, coming all the way from California."

"It is," I said, nodding. "But it's a good change. I needed something quieter."

"You came to the right place," Candice said, bagging my groceries. "Not much happens here, but that's part of the charm. Though I'm sure the hospital will keep you busy."

"That's what I've heard," I replied, smiling.

Candice leaned in slightly, her voice dropping to a conspiratorial tone. "You know, the hospital's got quite a history. Some folks say the Old Wing is still... well, let's just say it has its quirks."

I raised an eyebrow, intrigued. "Quirks?"

She shrugged with a knowing smile. "Every old building does. But don't let it bother you. It's a good hospital, and the people there are like family."

I nodded, filing away her words as I thanked her and picked up my bags. The detail lingered in my mind, adding another layer of curiosity to the place I'd just started calling home.

With my groceries stashed in the car, I decided to find something warm to drink. The chill of the morning was still clinging to me, and a cup of coffee sounded like the perfect remedy. A few blocks away, I stopped at a small coffee shop with a sign that read "The Warm Nook."

The shop lived up to its name. As soon as I stepped inside, I smelled the rich aroma of freshly brewed coffee and the warm glow of Edison bulbs strung across the ceiling. Wooden shelves lined the walls, filled with books of every genre, their spines invitingly worn. A fireplace crackled softly in the corner, and mismatched chairs surrounded rustic wooden tables. It felt less like a business and more like stepping into someone's living room.

The counter was operated by a cheerful barista with short, curly hair and an apron dusted with flour. "Morning," she greeted. "What can I get for you?"

"A latte, please," I said, scanning the chalkboard menu above her head. "And maybe one of those breakfast sandwiches?"

"Good choice," she said, grabbing a plate. "Fresh out of the oven this morning."

I found a seat near the fireplace, setting my coffee and scone on the table. The warmth of the fire was soothing, and I allowed myself a moment to take it all in. It had been so long since I'd felt this kind of peace.

As I took my first sip of coffee, the door chimed, and a lady walked in. Her auburn hair was tied back in a loose braid, and she had the kind of effortless confidence that made her stand out.

"Lila?" she said, spotting me. "Mind if I join you? I am Rowan, one of the ER nurses. I saw you come in yesterday"

"Of course," I said, gesturing to the chair across from me.

She placed her order at the counter before sitting down with a steaming mug of coffee. "Small town," she said with a grin. "You can't go anywhere without running into someone you know."

"I'm starting to see that," I replied, laughing softly. "But I kind of like it. It's... different."

"Different from California, I bet," Rowan said, leaning back in her chair. "What made you decide to come all the way out here?"

I hesitated for a moment before answering. "I... I needed a change. Things were... intense at my last job. I wanted somewhere quieter, where I could breathe."

Rowan nodded, her expression understanding. "I get that. Nightfall Pines has a way of growing on you. It's not perfect, but it's home."

We sipped our coffee in comfortable silence for a moment before Rowan spoke again. "So, what do you think of the hospital so far?"

"It's... different," I said honestly. "But in a good way. The people seem nice, and the pace is slower than what I'm used to. Luis has been great about showing me around."

Rowan smiled. "Luis is the best. He'll talk your ear off, but he's solid in a crisis. The whole team is, really. We're a small group but have each other's backs."

I nodded, taking in her words. It was reassuring to hear, especially as the new person trying to find her footing.

"What about the Old Wing?" I asked, lowering my voice slightly. "Candice at the grocery store mentioned something about it having... quirks."

Rowan's expression shifted slightly, "The Old Wing..." she began, trailing off. "It's just a relic of the past. It used to be part of the hospital, but about 50 years ago, there was a fire, and part of it burned down. No one really goes in there anymore."

"Why not?" I pressed gently.

She hesitated before answering. "Honestly? It's probably just superstition. You know how small towns are. Stories get passed down, and next thing you know, everyone thinks the place is haunted."

I laughed lightly, though her words only added to my curiosity. "Haunted, huh? Guess I'll have to see for myself."

Rowan smirked, but there was a hint of seriousness in her. "Just stick to the parts of the hospital you're supposed to be in. Trust me."

Her words hung in the air longer than I expected, the tone of her voice making me feel like there was more behind them. But I decided not to press further. Instead, I sipped my coffee and shifted the conversation.

Rowan leaned back in her chair, swirling her coffee idly. "So, you've probably already heard about Dr. Thomas Pike," she said, her tone casual but edged with curiosity.

I shook my head. "Not yet. Who is he?"

She smirked faintly. "He's the head doctor at the hospital. Been here forever—practically part of the furniture at this point. He's a brilliant physician, no doubt about that, but... let's just say he's a little intimidating."

"Intimidating how?" I asked, intrigued.

Rowan hesitated as if choosing her words carefully. "He's quiet, reserved. Doesn't talk much unless it's about work. Some of the newer staff are terrified of him, but I think it's just his personality. He's not unkind, just… hard to read."

She took a sip of her coffee before continuing. "I heard from one of the staff that his wife left him years ago. She vanished one day, supposedly running off with someone else. He's got a grown-up daughter, but she doesn't live here. Honestly, it's kind of sad."

I frowned, the story stirring an unexpected pang of empathy. "That must've been hard for him."

"Yeah," Rowan agreed, her tone softening. "But he doesn't talk about it, and no one dares to ask. He's devoted to the hospital, though. You'll see—he's always the first one in and the last one out."

I nodded and thought, *I've met plenty of doctors at my previous job with God complexes—those who would yell at you or respond in a condescending tone. I've dealt with that my entire nursing career. Quiet and reserved? I can handle that.*

"So, what do you do when you're not at the hospital?" I asked, hoping to steer things to a lighter topic.

Rowan relaxed slightly and smiled. "Oh, the usual small-town things. Hiking, reading, and trying out every item on the menu here at The Warm Nook and Thai Tasty. What about you? Any hobbies?"

I thought about it for a moment. It had been so long since I'd had the time or energy to think about hobbies. "I used to love reading," I said, glancing at the bookshelves around us. "Maybe this town will give me the chance to pick it back up."

"You came to the right place," Rowan said, gesturing to the shelves. "This coffee shop also doubles as a mini library. You can borrow anything you see here. Just jot it down in the notebook by the counter."

"Really? That's amazing," I said, making a mental note to browse the shelves before leaving.

Our conversation flowed easily after that. Rowan shared stories about the town's quirky festivals and traditions, and I found myself laughing more than I had in months. She made me feel at ease like I'd known her for years instead of just a day.

As we finished our coffee, Rowan glanced at her watch. "I should probably head out. Got a shift tonight. But hey, if you ever need a tour guide for the town—or someone to grab coffee with—I'm around. I'll see you tomorrow night, yeah?"

"Thanks, Rowan," I said, genuinely grateful. "I might take you up on that."

She gave me a warm smile before heading toward the door. As she left, the shop seemed a little quieter, though still inviting. I stayed a while longer, savoring the atmosphere and flipping through a book I'd pulled from the shelf. It felt like a small but significant step toward finding my place here.

Nightfall Pines, I think I like it here.

CHAPTER THREE: FIRST NIGHT HIGH

The hospital was quiet—eerily so—as I walked into the brightly lit emergency department. It was a different kind of silence than I was used to, one filled with the tension of potential chaos. The hum of fluorescent lights buzzed faintly above, and the distant beeping of monitors provided a steady rhythm to the otherwise still environment.

Luis greeted me at the nurses' station, his ever-present grin making me feel a little more at ease. What's a hospital without a Filipino nurse, "Ready for your first night shift?" he asked with a slightly thick accent.

Filipinos are the warmest. My stepmother was half-Filipino and came into my life when I was three, a year after my real mom passed away. She was also a nurse, and she's the one who encouraged me to become one. Sometimes, I wonder if I made the right choice. Why did I even choose this path? But she made it look so easy. She was caring, emphatic, and smart. I looked up to her. She took care of me like I was her own. She's very kind and very loving. God, I miss her. But now she's gone...She was gone right before my eyes, then she was....

"As ready as I'll ever be," I replied, forcing a smile while trying not to think about my stepmom. My stomach churned, not from the coffee but from the nervous energy coursing through me. It was strange. I'd been a nurse for five years, working in one of the busiest trauma centers in California, but tonight felt different. There was a weight in the air, a sense that this night was going to test me.

Luis must have sensed my nerves because he tapped me on the shoulder. "You've got this. We're a team here. And besides, it's usually quiet until midnight."

The word "quiet" was like a jinx in any emergency room, and I gave him a skeptical look. He laughed. "Okay, okay. Maybe I shouldn't have said that. Let me give you the grand tour before things pick up."

He walked me through the setup of the ER. It was smaller than what I was used to, with only eight patient bays and a modest trauma room equipped with the basics. The crash cart sat neatly in the corner, fully stocked with emergency medications and intubation supplies; the pyxis machine was on the left-hand side near the trauma room. Luis pointed out the O_2 connectors, the defibrillator's placement, and the Ambu bag hanging just above the patient's bed. Everything was within arm's reach, efficient, and well-organized.

"Dr. Harold Patel is leading tonight," Luis said as we passed the doctors' lounge. "He's one of the best. He is young and new, but he knows his stuff."

"Good to know," I said, trying to keep my voice steady. Internally, I was running through a mental checklist, ensuring I was prepared for anything that might roll through those doors. Still, doubt lingered in the back of my mind. Did I still have what it took to handle an emergency? Could I keep up after being away from this kind of chaos for a while and after... my last shift?

My thoughts were interrupted by the sound of wheels squeaking against the floor. A paramedic burst through the double doors, pushing a stretcher with a patient who was eerily still.

"Incoming! Female, mid-twenties found unresponsive at a church wedding venue fire. Full thickness burns over her body. No pulse. We've been doing compressions for ten minutes."

My mind raced: *Can I still do this? Am I ready for this again?*

I froze. The sight of the woman hitting me like a punch to the chest. Her body was charred, the once-pristine fabric of a wedding gown clinging to her frail, burned form. The edges of the dress were blackened, tattered like ghostly remnants of a moment that should have been filled with joy. Her veil, now a ragged shroud, clung stubbornly to her head, fluttering slightly with the movement of the stretcher. It was surreal, like something out of a nightmare.

My gaze fell to her left hand. A gold wedding ring glinted faintly under the harsh fluorescent lights, untouched by the flames, as though it refused to let go of the promises made that day. The sight of it twisted something deep inside me. This wasn't just a patient. This was a bride—a woman who had likely walked down the aisle only hours ago, surrounded by love and laughter, her life stretching out before her like a beautiful dream. And now? Now she was here, her life reduced to broken breaths and fading hope.

Her hair, or what little remained of it, was scorched, sticking in brittle patches to her scalp. A single shoe clung to her foot; the delicate satin melted and twisted, the sole blackened by fire. It was the kind of detail that shouldn't matter, but it did. It spoke of the person she was and the care she had taken to prepare for her day. Now, all that care, all that joy, had been replaced by this—a tragedy too unbearable to process.

The acrid smell of smoke and burnt fabric filled the air. I could also smell the metallic tang of blood mixed with betadine. It was overwhelming and suffocating, and for a moment, I couldn't move. My mind screamed at me to do something, to step forward, to help, but I was paralyzed by the sheer weight of what I was seeing.

I thought of her family, her groom—God, her groom. Was he waiting somewhere, praying for a miracle? Or was he lying in another hospital, unaware of what had happened to her? The questions came unbidden, flooding my mind with a mix of grief and helplessness.

"Lila!" Luis's voice cut through the fog, sharp and commanding. I blinked and turned to him, my hands trembling as he thrust a pair of gloves into them. "Focus. We've got this."

I nodded, forcing my feet to move, forcing the nurse in me to take over. There was no room for hesitation now. No time to feel the unbearable sadness pressing down on my chest. This was what I was trained for. This was why I was here.

I joined the team at the trauma bay, my training taking over. Dr. Patel was already there, his calm but commanding voice cutting through the tension. "Let's intubate. Push 1 milligram of epi. Lila, take over compressions."

I nodded, stepping into position. My hands pressed against her chest, and I began counting in my head. "One, two, three, four..." The rhythm was automatic, but my mind screamed with every compression at a rate of about 100 to 120 per minute. *What if I mess up? What if I'm not good enough? My adrenaline keeps me going.*

The burn victim's body felt fragile beneath my hands, but I kept going, focusing on the numbers. Luis handed the Ambu bag to Maggie, and she squeezed it rhythmically, watching her chest rise and fall. I could hear Dr. Patel's voice in the background, directing Rowan to administer medications and prepare the defibrillator.

"Patient is in V-fib, charging to 360 joules," someone called out.

The sound of the defibrillator charging felt like it lasted more than a minute, though it was only seconds.

"Clear!" Dr. Patel said, and the patient's body jerked slightly from the shock. Still no pulse. Asystole... The cycle continued: compressions, ambu bag, epinephrine... My muscles burned, but I didn't stop. Luis and I alternated chest compression, and we did not stop. I could not stop. Not until we had done everything we could.

Finally, after what felt like an eternity, Dr. Patel checked his watch. His voice was steady but heavy with finality. "Time of death: 21:34."

I stepped back, my chest heaving as I pulled off my gloves. My hands were trembling, and the room felt unbearably quiet. I glanced at the burnt remains of the young woman on the bed, her face barely recognizable. A wave of emotion threatened to break through, but I shoved it down, reminding myself that there was still work to do.

"Good job, everyone," Dr. Patel said, his tone clinical. He gave me a nod, a subtle acknowledgment of my efforts, before leaving the room.

Later, I sat at the nurses' station, the glow of the computer screen illuminating my tired face as I charted the events of the code. It's just a few minutes past midnight, and I still have a few more hours till my shift is over. The details were all in my head: time of arrival, medications administered, fluids, number of shocks, and time of death. But my thoughts were anything but mechanical.

Was there something else I could have done? I wondered. The doubts clawed at me, even though I knew rationally that we had done everything possible. It was the curse of the job, carrying the weight of every life lost.

"You did good there, you know."

The voice startled me, and I turned to see a woman leaning casually against the counter. Her eyes were kind, her presence was very motherly.

"I'm Evelyn," she said, "One of the nurse supervisors here."

"Thanks," I said quietly. "It's been a while since I've been in the thick of it."

"Could've fooled me," Evelyn said with a small smile. "You handled yourself well. Most people freeze for a lot longer on their first day."

I chuckled weakly. "I did freeze for a second there."

"But you didn't stay frozen," Evelyn countered. "That's what matters."

Her words were comforting, but I couldn't shake the weight in my chest. "It's hard not to second-guess everything," I admitted. "Even after all these years."

Evelyn nodded, pulling up a chair beside me. "I've been here a long time," she said. "Seen a lot of cases like tonight's. It never gets easier, but that's the thing about this job. We keep showing up, doing what we can."

We sat in silence for a moment, the only sound coming from the soft clicking of the keyboard as I finished my charting. Finally, Evelyn broke the silence.

"Why'd you leave your last job?" she asked, her tone gentle but curious.

I hesitated, the memories rushing back. The chaos, the overwhelming sense of failure, the moment that had finally broken me, my last shift.... I couldn't tell her what happened... "I uhm... I needed a change," I said simply.

"Things got... too heavy. I thought a quieter place might help me find my footing again."

Evelyn studied me for a moment, her gaze steady. "Well, you've come to the right place. Nightfall Pines has a way of helping people find what they need. Even if it's not always what they expect."

Her words hung in the air, and I felt a strange sense of comfort in them. Maybe she was right. Maybe this small, unassuming hospital in the middle of nowhere was exactly what I needed to find myself again.

"Thanks, Evelyn," I said, offering her a small smile.

"Anytime," she replied, standing to leave. "Get some rest. You'll need it."

As she walked away, I felt a sense of hope. Maybe I didn't have all the answers yet but tonight had proven that I still had the fight in me. And for now, that was enough.

By the end of the shift, I was running on fumes. My eyes felt heavy, and my hair had fallen out of its neat ponytail, now hanging limply over my shoulders. I stifled a yawn as I sat at the nurses' station, trying to finish up my charting. The clock on the wall ticked louder in the quiet ER, reminding me that I still had a few more details to document before I could call it a night.

The rest of the team was just as drained as I was. Luis leaned against the counter, sipping what looked like his third cup of coffee of the night. Despite the exhaustion written on his face, he still managed a grin. "First night shift down, Lila. You killed it."

I gave him a tired smile. "Barely. I feel like I've run a marathon."

Across from us, Rowan stretched her arms above her head, her braid swaying as she yawned. "You'll get used to it. Or you won't. Either way, welcome to the night shift."

Maggie, ever composed, chuckled softly. "This was a calm night by Nightfall standards. My first shift here? Total disaster. We had half the town in here for a flu outbreak. It's all uphill from there."

Dr. Patel walked by, his lab coat open and his stethoscope slung loosely around his neck. Even after a full shift, his steps were steady and confident. "Good job tonight, everyone," he said, his voice even as always. "Let's hope the day crew has a peaceful one."

I glanced at the patient bays. Only two were occupied now: one with a man recovering from a minor car accident and another with a woman who'd come in severely dehydrated. The earlier chaos of the night had dissolved into a calm, almost serene quiet. It was hard to believe the same space had been so frantic just hours ago.

After giving my report to the day shift nurse, I finally sat back and let out a deep breath. It felt good to hand over the reins, but I still had a little charting to finish before I could leave.

Luis swung his bag over his shoulder as he passed me. "You heading out?"

"Not yet," I said, rubbing the back of my neck. "Just need to chart few more things."

"Don't stay too long," Rowan chimed in with a tired laugh. "Trust me, you'll hate yourself when it's time to wake up tomorrow."

"Noted," I replied, managing a weak smile.

One by one, they said their goodbyes, leaving me alone in the ER. The space felt bigger without the rest of the crew around, the sound of monitors and the distant murmur of the day shift staff filling the silence. I made my way to the dictation room, the glow of the computer lighting up the dark space as I settled into the chair.

I started typing, my fingers moving sluggishly over the keyboard. My thoughts drifted as I filled in the details of the code earlier. The burnt bride. The image of her haunted me, and I couldn't stop replaying the scene in my head. The smell of burnt fabric, the sight of her charred veil.

I froze. The smell of burnt fabric was no longer just in my memory. I could smell it now. It was faint but unmistakable, acrid and clinging to the back of my throat. My heart skipped a beat, and I instinctively looked around the small room. It was empty, of course, but the smell lingered, growing stronger.

I shook my head, trying to focus. *You're imagining things,* I told myself, but the scent refused to fade. My hands faltered over the keyboard, and a strange sensation crept up the back of my neck like I was being watched.

I glanced up at the screen. My breath caught.

There, reflected on the dark edge of the monitor, was a figure standing behind me. The burnt bride. Her tattered gown hung loosely over her scorched body, and the remnants of her veil framed her face. The sight of her gold wedding ring glinting faintly in the monitor's glow made my blood run cold.

I froze, unable to move; my breath caught somewhere between a gasp and a scream. My pulse thundered in my ears as I tried to convince myself it wasn't real. *It's just your mind playing tricks on you. It has to be.*

I forced myself to turn around, but the room was empty. The chair behind me sat undisturbed, the air still and quiet. The smell of burnt fabric lingered, faint now, but still present.

My chest heaved as I struggled to calm down, but the lingering feeling of being watched refused to leave.

I turned back to the computer, hastily saving my work before shutting it down. My hands were trembling as I grabbed my bag and rushed out of the dictation room. The moment I stepped into the hallway, I glanced over my shoulder, half-expecting to see her again. But the corridor was empty.

"Get it together, Lila," I muttered under my breath, my voice shaky. But no matter how much I tried to rationalize it, the image of the burnt bride standing behind me wouldn't leave my mind.

I turned off the computer, my hands trembling as I gathered my things. The faint smell of burnt fabric still lingered, clinging to the air like an unwelcome reminder of what I'd just seen. My heart raced as I stepped into the hallway, the fluorescent lights above casting long, flickering shadows. I needed to get to the locker room, grab my stuff, and leave—just get out of here before my mind played any more tricks on me.

The hallway felt longer than usual, every footstep echoing in the silence. I clutched my bag tightly, trying to steady my breathing. I could do this. I just needed to get to the end of the hall. One step at a time.

Then, as I reached for my ID badge clipped to my pocket, my pen slipped from my fingers and clattered to the floor. I knelt to pick it up, but when I looked up, I froze.

She was there.

Standing no more than a foot in front of me, the burnt bride loomed in the dim hallway, her charred gown hanging off her scorched frame. Her face—God, her face. The flesh was blackened and peeling, her empty eye sockets staring straight into mine. The remnants of her veil framed her head like a grotesque crown, and her cracked lips parted as if she were about to speak.

Then she began to move.

Her steps were slow, deliberate, and impossibly silent. The hem of her burned gown dragged across the floor as she closed the distance between us. I couldn't breathe. My pulse thundered in my ears, and my body refused to move. Her lifeless gaze bore into me, and I swore I could hear faint whispers, like the hiss of smoke and flame.

"No," I whispered, shaking my head. "No, no, no..."

My voice grew louder as panic took hold. "Stay back!" I cried, my words echoing down the empty hallway. I scrambled backward, pressing myself against the cold wall. "You're not real! You can't be real!"

The smell of smoke was overwhelming now, choking me as I gasped for air. My hands clutched at the wall, desperate for some kind of anchor, but there was nothing to ground me. My vision blurred with tears as I watched her come closer, her figure impossibly steady and hauntingly calm.

"Please! Stay away!" I screamed, the hysteria in my voice rising as I shook uncontrollably. I wanted to run, but my legs felt like lead. All I could do was watch in terror as she kept coming, her scorched frame illuminated by the flickering hallway lights.

I buried my face in my hands, sobbing uncontrollably. "Go away, go away, go away..." The words tumbled out in a broken plea, muffled against my trembling fingers. My entire body shook as I curled into myself, unable to face her any longer.

And then, as suddenly as it began, the air grew still. The suffocating scent of smoke faded, replaced by the sterile smell of the hospital. The hallway fell silent, and I could feel the emptiness around me.

Slowly, I lifted my head, tears streaming down my face. The burnt bride was gone. The hallway was empty.

I sat there for what felt like hours, my chest heaving with every ragged breath. My hands trembled as I pushed myself up, clutching the wall for support. My pen lay on the floor, but I couldn't bring myself to pick it up.

She had been real. I knew it in my bones. She wasn't just a trick of my mind. She had been there, walking toward me, and she had seen me.

And now, I knew she wouldn't be the last.

CHAPTER FOUR: A GIFT OR A CURSE

I ran into the janitor's closet. It was cramped and dimly lit, the faint smell of cleaning chemicals mixing with the musty scent of old mop heads. I sat on the floor; knees pulled tightly to my chest and buried my face in my hands. My breaths came in short, uneven gasps, my heart still pounding as though it wanted to escape my chest. I couldn't stop shaking. The image of the burnt bride—her scorched face, her hollow eyes—was burned into my mind, as vivid as if she were still standing right in front of me.

The sound of the door creaking open made me jolt. I wiped my face hastily, trying to compose myself, though my hands wouldn't stop trembling.

"Lila?" Evelyn's voice was soft, concerned. She stepped inside, closed the door behind her, and crouched to meet my gaze. "What are you doing in here?"

I shook my head, unable to find the words. My throat felt tight, like I might choke if I tried to speak.

Evelyn didn't push. She simply sat down on the floor beside me, her presence steady and grounding. "I've seen that look before," she said after a moment, her tone gentle. "Something happened. Talk to me."

I hesitated; the words caught somewhere between my heart and my lips. I didn't want to tell her. I didn't want to admit that I might be losing my mind. But the kindness in her eyes was impossible to ignore, and before I could stop myself, the truth started spilling out.

"I saw her," I whispered, my voice shaking. "The burnt bride. I saw her... twice."

Evelyn's brows furrowed slightly, but she didn't interrupt.

"She was behind me in the dictation room. And then..." My voice cracked, and I swallowed hard, forcing myself to continue. "And then I saw her again in the hallway. She was... she was walking toward me. I... I couldn't move. I couldn't breathe. It was like she was there for me."

Evelyn's expression softened, but there was something unreadable in her eyes. "You're not crazy, Lila. I believe you."

Tears spilled down my eyes uncontrollably. I didn't know if it was the relief of being believed or the sheer weight of everything I'd been holding in, but the dam broke, and I couldn't stop the sobs that followed.

Evelyn placed a hand on my shoulder, firm but comforting. "You've been through something, haven't you?" she asked quietly. "Something more than just moving to a new town or starting a new job. What brought you here, Lila? What made you leave your last hospital?"

I stiffened, the memories I'd tried so hard to bury rushing back all at once. My hands clenched into fists on my lap, and my breath hitched. For a long moment, I couldn't speak. Then, finally, the words came, slow and fractured.

"It was supposed to be a normal shift," I began, my voice barely audible. "Just like any other shift but this time was different."

Evelyn didn't say anything, but her presence urged me to keep going.

It was a warm summer day, one of those deceptive days where the world seemed calm, yet chaos was waiting just around the corner.

I had been on the day shift, wearing my favorite pale blue scrubs—the ones my stepmom had given me for my first nursing job. My alarm did not go off that morning for some reason, so I had to rush going to work. I was late. I remember the sound of patient call lights, the monitor, and the IV pumps going off. It's like a backdrop sound to the chaos that followed. But that day, it was nothing more than noise. The kind of noise you stop noticing when adrenaline takes over.

The call came in: a severe car accident, collision at the intersection, one severely injured. My pulse quickened, as it always did in these moments. This was what I'd trained for, what I'd done countless times. I was ready—or so I thought.

Then, the paramedics rolled in.

At first, I didn't recognize her. The blood, the bruises, the unnatural stillness—all of it made her look like a stranger. But then I saw her necklace, the one I'd helped her clasp on my graduation day. My heart dropped into my stomach. It felt like the ground beneath me had vanished, leaving me suspended in a free fall.

The room spun around me as I stood frozen in place. My colleagues moved with precision, shouting vitals and updates as they worked on her. Someone called for a crash cart. I hear the cardiac monitor when it's in asystole, a sound I knew so well but now felt like a knife twisting in my chest.

I couldn't move. I couldn't speak. My best friend Sarah, who was on shift with me that day, grabbed my arm and tried to lead me out of the room. "Lila, you don't have to watch this," she had said, her voice soft but firm.

But I couldn't leave. How could I?

The woman on that stretcher wasn't just another patient. She was my stepmom, Melissa, the only mother I'd ever really known. The only woman who stood up for me, who took me to every dance recital, who cheered for me at every graduation, who showed up when my dad couldn't.

The woman whom I met when I was three, who loved me since then even though I wasn't hers to love.

So, I stayed. I stayed and watched as the team fought to save her. I watched as the monitor showed her heart rhythm fading, as the compressions became more desperate. I watched as they pushed Epi, as they shocked her, as they pumped her chest over and over and over again... I knew the rhythm of the compressions and the sound of the defibrillator while it was charging. I knew every step they were taking because I'd done it a hundred times before. But this time... this time, I was just in the corner.

The minutes stretched on like hours. I couldn't hear anything but the sound of my own heartbeat roaring in my ears. My vision blurred, but I didn't blink. I couldn't look away.

I swallowed hard, the lump in my throat making it hard to continue as I remember the worst day of my life.

The ER doctor shook his head multiple times, and I begged him to do another round of CPR.

And then it happened.

"Time of death," the doctor said, his voice heavy with finality. The words hit me like a physical blow. My knees buckled, but I stayed upright, clutching the edge of the counter for support. My mind screamed, but no sound came out.

The team began cleaning up, their faces somber but detached. This was routine for them, just another tragic case in the ER. But for me, it was the end of my world.

I turned away, my body trembling uncontrollably. I needed air. I needed to get out. But as I took a step toward the door, I felt it—the inexplicable sensation of being watched.

I froze as I held my breath. Slowly, I turned, and there she was.

She was standing right behind me, her body bloody and broken, just as it had been on the stretcher. Her eyes were wide and unseeing, her mouth slightly open as if she were trying to speak. My heart pounded so loudly I thought it might burst.

"Lila," she said, her voice twisted and broken, echoing as though it came straight from a nightmare. "Am I dead?"

I couldn't answer. My voice, my breath—everything had abandoned me. I stumbled backward, my hands gripping the doorframe for support. The room around me seemed to fade, leaving only her and the unbearable weight of her question.

"Lila," she repeated, her voice growing more desperate. "Am I dead?"

I don't remember screaming, but I know I did. It was the kind of scream that tore through your throat, primal and raw. Someone must have pulled me out of the room because the next thing I knew, I was in the staff lounge, gasping for air, my vision blurred with tears.

That day was the last time I saw her, alive and dead. But her voice—her face—has never left me. It lingers in the quiet moments, in the spaces between breaths, a constant reminder of the one question I never answered.

All I remember is her face and voice and how she looked at me like she was begging me for answers I didn't have.

"Am I dead?"

The silence that followed was heavy, broken only by my uneven breaths. Evelyn didn't speak immediately, giving me the space to process my words.

"And then I quit," I said finally. "I couldn't go back. Every time I closed my eyes, I saw her. Every time I walked into a patient room, I heard her voice. I thought moving here, to a quiet town, would help. That maybe I could leave it all behind and start fresh."

Evelyn nodded slowly. "But you can't outrun something like that," she said gently. "Maybe you were never meant to."

I looked at her, confusion and desperation mixing in my tear-streaked face. "What does that mean?"

She hesitated as if choosing her words carefully. "Some people see things, Lila. Things most of us can't. Maybe it's a gift. Maybe it's a curse. But whatever it is, it's yours. And running from it won't make it go away."

Her words lingered, settling deep in my chest. "You see them because they're asking for help. Maybe they're drawn to you because they know you can hear them. Maybe that's why it's always been you."

I stared at her, her words sinking in, but my mind couldn't stop racing. "What do you mean 'always'? This just... started happening."

Evelyn's expression softened further, almost as if she had expected my denial. "Are you sure about that, Lila? Think back. Think hard."

Her words hit me like a jolt, unlocking a door I hadn't opened in years. Memories I had buried deep rushed forward, unbidden.

"I was five," I said, my voice barely a whisper. "Kindergarten. There was an empty classroom down the hall. I was walking back from the restroom when I saw her, a teacher."

Evelyn nodded encouragingly but stayed silent, letting me speak.

"She was standing in the doorway," I continued, my voice trembling. "She looked normal at first, like any other teacher. She smiled and gestured for me to come closer. I remember thinking she must have needed help with something."

I swallowed hard, my hands clenching into fists on my lap. "But as I walked closer, I saw it. Her stomach... it was bleeding. A deep, dark stain spread across her blouse. And then she looked at me, her eyes filled with pain, and said, 'Help me.'"

The memory made my breath hitch, the raw terror as vivid as the day it happened. "I screamed and ran. I didn't stop until I reached the teacher on duty. They said there was no one in that classroom. I didn't speak for weeks after that. My parents had to hire a therapist to help me."

I hesitated, my heart pounding as Evelyn's words stirred another memory I hadn't thought about in years. "It wasn't just in kindergarten," I admitted quietly. "Something happened when I was in nursing school, too."

Evelyn tilted her head, her expression both curious and patient. "What happened?"

"It was during my first clinical in the Med-Surg unit," I began, my voice trembling slightly. "We were each assigned rooms to check on during our shift. I wasn't assigned to room 3107, but the call light for that room kept going off. Nobody else seemed to notice it, and I thought maybe the assigned nurse had missed it, so I went in."

I could still see it in my mind: the stark, sterile hallway, the bright fluorescent light, and the small, illuminated number plate on the door that read *3107*. "As I opened the door and walked in, I saw him. A thin, frail man sitting on the edge of the bed, his legs dangling. His skin was pale, almost translucent, and he had deep, sunken eyes. He looked like he hadn't eaten in weeks."

I swallowed hard, my voice dropping as I recounted the eerie moment. "I asked him, 'Do you need anything?' And he just looked at me with those hollow eyes and said, 'I want water. I'm very thirsty.' His voice—it wasn't normal. It was raspy, like it came from somewhere deep, almost echoing."

Evelyn leaned closer; her brows furrowed. "What did you do?"

"I told him I'd check with the nurse to make sure he wasn't NPO," I said, shaking my head as the memory unfolded. "I didn't want to give him water without confirming, so I looked for one of my classmates. When I found him, I said, 'Your patient in room 3107 wants water.'"

Evelyn's eyes widened slightly as if she already knew where the story was going.

"My classmate just stared at me," I continued. "He said, '3107? Are you sure? There's no one in that room.'"

I felt a chill run down my spine, the memory as vivid now as it had been then. "I thought he was messing with me, so I made him come back with me to check. But when we opened the door, the room was empty. Completely empty. No patient, no signs anyone had been there."

I paused, my breath hitching as the realization hit me all over again. "I looked around the room, checked under the bed, and even opened the closet. But there was nothing. My classmate laughed it off and said I must have been imagining things. But I know what I saw. He was there."

Evelyn nodded slowly, her gaze unwavering. "And you never told anyone else?"

"No," I whispered. "I thought maybe I was just overtired that I was seeing things because of the stress. But now..." I trailed off, my mind racing.

"But now," Evelyn said gently, "You're starting to realize it's not just coincidence. Lila, they've been reaching out to you your whole life. And every time, they need something. Help, closure, acknowledgment. That's why you see them."

I sat there, my hands trembling, as the weight of her words settled over me. This wasn't just random. This wasn't just some cruel twist of fate. It was something more. And it terrified me.

Evelyn said firmly, "Lila, this has always been with you. You have a gift, whether you like it or not. You see these things because they need you. The burnt bride, the others— they're coming to you because they know you can help."

"But I don't want this," I said, tears streaming down my face. "It's not a gift. It's a curse."

Evelyn sighed, her gaze steady. "Maybe it feels that way now. But gifts often do, until we learn how to use them. You have a choice, Lila. You can run from it, let it consume you, or you can face it. Learn how to control it. Learn how to help."

Her words struck something deep within me, a mixture of fear and hope that I couldn't quite untangle. I didn't know if I could do what she suggested, but I felt a faint glimmer of possibility for the first time.

"I don't know how," I whispered. "I don't even know where to start."

"You'll figure it out," Evelyn said, her voice kind but certain. "And you won't have to do it alone. You do not have to fear."

I just stared at her for a moment, the weight of her words settling over me. Maybe I couldn't run from this anymore. Maybe it was time to stop being afraid.

Evelyn stood, offering me her hand. "Come on. Let's get out of this closet. You've got a lot to think about."

I took her hand, her grip strong and reassuring. As we stepped into the quiet hallway, I felt the smallest sliver of resolve beginning to form. I didn't have all the answers yet, but maybe, just maybe, I could find them.

CHAPTER FIVE: THE BURNT BRIDE

The doors of Nightfall Pines Regional Hospital creeks as I stepped inside for another shift. The air inside carried that familiar, sterile hospital smell. I took a deep breath, shaking off the lingering chill of the evening.

Jerry was mopping the floors near the entrance, his usual cheerful energy on full display. "Good evening, Lila!" he said, pausing mid-swipe. "Ready for another fun-filled night?"

I smirked at his enthusiasm. "If by fun, you mean chaos, then absolutely."

Jerry laughed, his mop slapping the tile with a playful flourish. "Chaos is the spice of life, isn't it? Don't let them work you too hard tonight, okay?"

"Only if you save me a spot in the janitor's closet," I teased before continuing down the hall.

The break room was alive with chatter when I walked in. Luis, Maggie, and Rowan were huddled at the table, nursing their pre-shift coffees. Luis was in the middle of what sounded like a wildly exaggerated story about a fishing trip gone wrong.

"Ah, California's here!" Luis announced as I stepped inside. "Tell me, Lila, are you a coffee-first kind of nurse or a let's-get-this-shift-over-with type?"

"Why can't I be both?" I said, dropping my bag into a chair and reaching for the coffee pot.

Maggie snorted. "You'll need it tonight. The bat guy isn't coming till tomorrow, but we've got a couple of gems waiting for us already."

"Bat guy?" I asked, eyebrows raised.

"Long story," Rowan said with a grin. "Let's just say the ER is never boring."

Before I could ask more, another nurse stuck her head into the room. "Lila? Dr. Pike wants to see you in his office."

A hush fell over the group for a second, and then Luis leaned back in his chair with a dramatic groan. "Ooh, the boss wants a word. Don't worry, it's probably not about you. Probably."

"Helpful as always, Luis," I muttered, my stomach tightening slightly.

The walk to Dr. Pike's office felt longer than it should have. I knocked lightly on the door before stepping in.

"Dr. Pike?"

The man sitting behind the desk looked up from a stack of papers, and I was immediately struck by how different he was from what I'd expected. He looked like he belonged in a medical journal photograph—tall, with neatly combed silver hair and glasses perched on a strong nose. But I was told he recently turned 75, he looked way younger. He had an air of quiet confidence that made you sit up straighter without meaning to.

"Lila," he said, standing and offering a hand. "Come in. Close the door."

I shook his hand and took a seat, trying not to fidget. His office was cluttered but not messy. Medical books with worn spines filled the shelves, their titles a mix of familiar and obscure. Papers and patient files were stacked on every available surface, and a single photo of a young woman—his daughter, I guessed—sat on his desk.

"I wanted to welcome you to Nightfall Pines officially," he said, his voice calm and measured. "I hope you're settling in well."

"I am," I replied. "It's been an adjustment, but everyone's been very welcoming."

Dr. Pike nodded. "That's good to hear. It's not easy to join a smaller hospital, especially from a place like California. But this team takes care of each other, and I have no doubt you'll fit right in."

His words were sincere, and they eased some of the nerves I hadn't realized I'd been carrying.

"Thank you," I said. "I'm looking forward to learning from everyone here."

He smiled faintly. "You'll find that Nightfall Pines has its quirks. But it's a good place. A place where people matter," "Just one rule: do not go to the Old Wing:" he continued.

"What about the old wing?" I curiously asked.

"Uhm, there's black molds. I do not want you getting sick," he said.

The conversation didn't last long, but by the time I left, I felt like I understood why everyone spoke so highly of him. He wasn't intimidating or condescending—he just had a quiet authority about him that commanded respect.

Back in the ER, Luis handed me a clipboard with my patient assignments. "You've got beds three and four. Start with three; it should be easy to warm up with."

I skimmed the chart for bed three: *40-year-old male, nausea and vomiting for two days. No fever.*

When I walked into the room, the patient was sitting on the edge of the bed, his shoulders hunched and his face pale. "Hi there," I said, offering a smile. "I'm Lila, and I'll be your nurse tonight. I see you've been feeling awful."

The man nodded weakly. "Yeah. Feels like I can't keep anything down."

"Well, let's see if we can fix that," I said, glancing at the orders. "We can give you something for the nausea, but we'll need to start an IV first. Is that okay?"

He nodded again. "Yeah, whatever works."

I pulled on gloves and grabbed the supplies I needed. "Okay, I'm going to use a 20-gauge needle for this. One quick poke and you'll be good to go."

I wrapped the tourniquet around his arm and palpated for a vein, finding one quickly. With one smooth motion, I inserted the needle, secured the IV, and started a normal saline bag.

"You're a pro," he said, his voice tinged with relief. "Didn't even feel that."

I smiled as I adjusted the flow rate. "Good. That's what I like to hear."

Once the IV was set, I pushed 4 mg of Zofran as ordered and made sure he was comfortable before heading back to the nurses' station. The shift was just beginning, but something about the calm made me nervous.

Something was coming. I could feel it.

I was in the middle of checking on another patient when I noticed the curtain in the ER bay nearest to the automatic doors fluttering. The draft from the doors was normal, but what caught my attention wasn't the movement—it was what was underneath the curtain. Two legs. Floating. Not touching the floor. One shoe was barely clinging to a foot; the other shoe was missing.

My stomach turned as I froze in place. I recognized those legs.

It was her.

The Burnt Bride.

My heart pounded in my chest, each beat reverberating in my ears. I forced myself to move toward the curtain, swallowing the lump in my throat. With trembling fingers, I grabbed the edge of the fabric and pulled it back.

Nothing. The bay was empty.

I exhaled shakily, trying to steady myself, but the air around me had turned icy. I couldn't see her, but I could feel her presence. My breath came out in soft puffs, visible in the chill. She was here. Watching. Waiting.

I pushed through the rest of my tasks, trying to shake off the unease. By the time I reached the bathroom to wash my face, the weight of the night was pressing down on me. It was close to midnight, and the fatigue of the shift was sinking into my bones. I splashed cold water on my face, hoping to shake the tension creeping up my spine.

When I looked up, she was there.

Her charred face stared back at me from the mirror, her hollow eyes locked onto mine. The wisps of her scorched veil floated in the air, almost ethereal, like smoke. I turned to face her, my legs trembling, my voice was unsteady as I forced myself to speak.

"What... what do you want?" I asked, barely above a whisper.

The Burnt Bride's veil brushed against my hand, and in an instant, I was no longer in the bathroom.

The air felt warm and light, perfumed with roses and candles. I was in a chapel, surrounded by golden light. The sound of the violin and the organ filled the air, blending with the quiet rustling of fabric as guests adjusted themselves on the pews. Everything was vibrant and alive, but I didn't feel like myself—I was just... there. Watching. Witnessing.

And there I saw a woman. Not scorching or haunting. A woman who smiles from ear to ear, her eyes shine like a star. She was beautiful. Her wedding dress flowed like clouds around her, delicate lace trailing behind her as she adjusted her veil. Her face was glowing, her smile wide and full of promise. Bridesmaids in blush-colored gowns surrounded her, fussing over small details—the hem of her dress, a stray curl of her hair. She was beaming, holding a small, folded piece of paper in her hands. Her vows. She tucked it in between her chest and dress as she tried to memorize it. "Just in case I forget a line," she exhaled.

I wanted to move closer, but I couldn't. It was as though I were tethered, only allowed to see what she wanted me to see. She walked down the aisle, and the groom was waiting for her. It was a glorious moment filled with tears and joy. A celebration of love and new beginnings.

There, I saw two people deeply in love, their eyes locked as if the rest of the world had ceased to exist. They looked at each other not just with affection but with the certainty of a shared future—a future they were about to step into together. The beautiful bride, radiant in her flowing gown, seemed to float with each step she took down the aisle. Her veil cascaded behind her like a soft whisper of hope, and her face glowed with a joy that could light even the darkest room.

The groom stood at the altar, his eyes glistening with unshed tears, his hands trembling slightly as he reached out to her. His love for her was so evident that it seemed to fill the room, wrapping around everyone present like a warm embrace. Every step she took toward him seemed to echo the promises they were about to make, promises of forever.

The ambiance was heavy with emotion, the kind that makes your heart swell and your throat tighten. I could hear the soft murmur of the guests, their smiles reflecting the happiness of the couple. Sunlight streamed through the stained-glass windows, painting the room in hues of amber and gold as if the heavens themselves were blessing this union.

As I watched the bride walk closer, I noticed her hands trembling slightly, clutching her bouquet as though it anchored her to this moment. Her eyes shone with tears, but they were tears of joy, of anticipation, of a love so profound that it could withstand anything.

The room seemed alive, not just with celebration, but with the collective hope of everyone present. It wasn't just a wedding—it was the embodiment of love conquering all, of two souls finding each other and choosing to walk together through life. This was a day of new beginnings, a moment where the past faded into irrelevance, leaving only the promise of a shared tomorrow.

And yet, there was something bittersweet about the scene. As much as joy and love filled the air, a faint undercurrent of fragility lingered, a quiet reminder of how fleeting these moments can be. I could feel my own eyes sting with tears, overwhelmed by the beauty and weight of it all. This wasn't just a union—it was a triumph of hope, a testament to the enduring power of love.

The bride reached the altar, her hand slipping into the groom, and the room seemed to hold its breath. This was their moment—a moment of promises, of faith, of two hearts becoming one. I found myself lost in the raw, unfiltered beauty of it all, grateful to witness a love so pure it could transcend time itself.

He took her hands and began to speak, his voice steady, his words full of devotion.

"I promise to stand by your side," he began, his voice full of quiet strength. "To share in your joy and your sorrow, to build a life with you that is filled with love and laughter. You are my heart, my home, my everything."

The words were simple but heartfelt, and as he put the ring onto her finger, her smile widened. Her cheeks flushed with emotion, and I could see tears glistening in her eyes.

It was her turn.

Then it happened.

A single candle tipped over at the back of the altar, the flame catching on the silk drapery. At first, no one noticed. The fire started small but grew quickly, swallowing the flowers and decorations like they were kindling. Panic rippled through the chapel as guests screamed and scrambled for the exits. Smoke began to fill the air, thick and suffocating.

I wanted to scream for her to run, but I couldn't. She stood frozen as chaos unfolded around her. Her dress caught fire, the flames licking at the delicate lace and climbing up toward her veil. She cried out, in her panic, she didn't see what I saw—the fire consuming everything, leaving nothing but ash and pain.

I gasped as I snapped back to reality, gripping the edge of the sink to steady myself. My reflection stared back at me, pale and wide-eyed, as my chest heaved with shallow breaths. My hands trembled as I try to make sense of what I had just seen.

Evelyn's voice echoed in my mind, soft and steady. *"Maybe it's a gift, Lila. Maybe you're seeing these things because they need your help."*

I closed my eyes and thought about the words she never got to say. Her unfinished business.

My fear hadn't gone away, but something else settled in its place. Determination. If this was a gift, then I couldn't ignore it anymore.

She needed my help.

After finishing my shift, I stayed behind in the hospital's storage area, where unclaimed belongings were kept. I searched through her file, finding the small box of personal items that had been stored. Inside were scorched pieces of fabric, a damaged hair clip, and tucked beneath everything— a slip of paper.

I unfolded it carefully, my hands trembling as I read the words. It was her vow. Written in neat, delicate handwriting, it was simple yet profound, filled with love and promises she never got to share. I knew then that I had to get it to someone who mattered to her.

I looked through her chart and found the emergency contact: Jacob. I called him, explaining only that we had some of her belongings that hadn't been picked up and asking if he could come to the hospital. He agreed.

When he arrived, I led him into a private room. He was a tall man with a weary look about him, his grief still fresh. I handed him the box, explaining that these were the last pieces of her life we had.

"She was beautiful," he said softly, holding the damaged hair clip in his hands. His voice cracked as he spoke. "I don't know how to move on."

I hesitated, my eyes flicking to the corner of the room where she stood, watching him. Tears streamed down her face, her lips moving silently as though she was trying to speak. He couldn't see her, but I could.

"There was something else," I said, carefully pulling out the piece of paper. "This was tucked into her gown."

I unfolded it and began to read aloud, my voice trembling as if it were her own. She recites her vow as I read it, although he couldn't hear her.

"My love, as I stand here today, I vow to be your partner in all things. I vow to love you in the quiet moments and the storms. To laugh with you, cry with you, and build a life that is ours. You are my greatest joy, my deepest comfort, and my truest friend. Today, I give you my heart completely, with no reservations, no fears, and no doubts. I am yours, forever and always, till death do us part."

The room was heavy with silence as I finished. Her husband's shoulders shook, and he buried his face in his hands, sobbing.

Behind him, the Burnt Bride was crying too, but her tears were different—soft, relieved. Her lips moved again, but I could hear her faint whisper this time.

"Thank you."

And then, as quickly as she appeared, she vanished like the wind, leaving only a faint light of the life she had and the memory of her etched forever in her husband's mind.

I never saw her again.

CHAPTER SIX: THE BOY WHO FOUND WORDS

The crisp autumn air wrapped around me as we climbed higher up the trail. Every step brought a new view with its towering pines and vibrant fall colors. The Oregon coast had its charm year-round, but in the fall, it felt like something out of a dream. The warm light filtered through the trees, painting the ground in different hues. Rowan walked ahead of me, her ponytail swaying, while Maggie followed close behind. We finally get a day off.

You okay back there, Lila?" Rowan called from ahead, her voice cutting through the serenity. She was leading the way, her pace brisk but not unkind.

"I'm fine," I replied, a little breathless. "Just soaking it all in."

"It's worth it, right?" Maggie chimed in, a cheerful bounce in her step as she caught up to Rowan. "Wait till you see the lake. This place is magic."

I smiled, feeling my shoulders relax for the first time in days. The hospital, the ghosts, the lingering tension of what I'd left behind—it all felt miles away up here. The smell of pine and earth filled the air, and the occasional rustle of leaves in the breeze was the only sound besides our footsteps.

The trail curved. The trees gave way to an expansive view of the lake, nestled in a quiet valley like a hidden gem. The water was still, a perfect mirror reflecting the vibrant foliage around it. Reds, oranges, yellows, and greens blended on the surface, creating a scene so beautiful it felt unreal.

"Wow," I breathed, stopping in my tracks to take it all in.

"Told you," Rowan said with a grin. She adjusted her ponytail and gestured toward the shore. "Come on, let's set up by the water."

We found a spot close to the lake's edge, spreading out a blanket and unpacking the snacks Rowan had brought. She poured coffee from a thermos into three mismatched mugs, handing one to me. I cradled it in my hands, savoring the warmth as I watched the sunlight dance on the water.

Maggie skipped stones. Rowan stretched out on the blanket, her arms behind her head, eyes closed. I let myself relax for a moment, the weight of the last few weeks lifting as I breathed in the crisp, clean air.

"I needed this," I said softly, almost to myself.

Rowan cracked one eye open and smirked. "Told you. The lake has that effect. It's like... therapy without the talking."

We laughed, and I let myself fall back onto the blanket, staring up at the patches of sky peeking through the trees.

But then, I guess I cannot get away from this gift or curse.

It started as a subtle chill, a strange cold that seemed to wrap around me. It wasn't a typical cold. It's that kind where it started at the back of my spine throughout my body. My skin prickled, and I sat up, glancing around. That's when I saw him.

A little boy stood just a few feet behind me, and his small frame was drenched, water dripping steadily from his clothes and pooling at his feet. His pale skin was almost translucent, and his lips were bluish-purple. His hair was in wet strands, and his eyes locked onto mine—wide and glassy, almost hollow.

"Have you seen my toy?" he asked, his voice soft and hollow. There was an echo to it, faint but unmistakable.

I froze as my breath was caught in my throat. My coffee wobbled in my hands, threatening to spill.

"What?" I managed to whisper, barely able to find my voice.

"My superhero toy," he repeated, taking a step closer. The water dripping from him left no marks on the ground, no indication that he was there.

"Lila?" Rowan's voice broke through the moment, startling me. "Are you okay?"

I blinked, tearing my eyes away from the boy. Rowan and Maggie were looking at me, their expressions curious but unconcerned. When I glanced back at the boy, he was still there, staring at me with that same eerie intensity.

"Yeah," I lied, my voice shaky. "I'm fine."

Rowan raised an eyebrow but shrugged, leaning back again. Maggie returned to skipping stones. I gripped my coffee tightly, my hands trembling as I looked back at the boy.

He tilted his head slightly, his gaze unblinking. He took a step closer with his bare feet. "I just want my toy," he said, his voice almost pleading.

I opened my mouth to respond, but before I could, I heard a scream.

"Matthew!" A woman's voice, shrill and panicked, echoed through the trees. "Matthew!!!!"

I whipped my head toward the sound, my heart pounding. A group of people had gathered across the lake near a cluster of rocks. A woman was kneeling on the ground, her hands pressing against the small, lifeless body of a boy. His skin was pale, his limbs limp, and his wet clothes clung to him.

The boy beside me turned toward the scene. His pale lips quivered, and his small hands clenched at his sides. I felt a lump rise in my throat as I realized what was happening. This boy, this ghost in front of me, was Matthew.

The group across the lake moved frantically. A man performed chest compressions while another shouted into a phone. The woman, Matthew's mother, I assumed—sobbed uncontrollably, her cries piercing the stillness. The three of us ran to help. Rowan took over compressions while Maggie pulled a piece of cloth to put a barrier between her mouth and the boy's mouth while giving breaths.

"Matthew, please," she begged, her hands trembling as she touched his face. "Please wake up. Please…"

The boy's ghostly figure didn't move, didn't speak. He just stared at the scene with a quiet sadness, his pale eyes reflecting the chaos around him.

My gaze shifted to the rocks near the water, where something bright and shiny caught my eye. A superhero toy. It lay half-buried among the stones, its bright colors vivid against the muted tones of the lake.

I stood slowly, my legs shaky as I walked toward it. The boy followed me; his translucent figure was like a candle flame. I bent down and picked up the toy, the plastic cool and damp in my hands.

The moment my fingers brushed against the toy, the world around me dissolved. The lake, the cool autumn air, and the sound of leaves rustling in the breeze all faded into a swirling haze. Then, as if through a lens clearing, I found myself in a different place and time.

There he was—the little boy. He couldn't have been more than five years old. He sat in the corner of a daycare, clutching his superhero toy tightly to his chest, his small frame curled into himself. Around him, the room buzzed with laughter and chatter from other children, but his world was different—it was fragmented, a mosaic of sounds and sights that didn't fit together in the way they did for everyone else.

He didn't hear the sounds as others did. To him, the laughter of other children wasn't comforting or inviting—it was jagged and harsh, like a sharp crack of thunder on a sunny day. It made him wince, his tiny hands pressing firmly against his ears as he hummed to himself, a soothing melody only he could understand.

I could feel his frustration, his yearning. His eyes darted around the room, filled with a longing to be part of the group, to run and play like the others. But the words he needed wouldn't come. They danced on the edge of his mind, elusive and taunting. Instead, only small, repetitive sounds emerged—hums, clicks, and soft groans. He wanted to explain himself, to tell the other children how much he loved his superhero toy, how his toy was his best friend, but no one would understand him. And so, he stayed quiet, retreating deeper into his own world.

His world was different—brighter, sharper. The colors of the toys around him weren't just vibrant; they screamed for attention. The texture of the carpet under his small fingers was too rough, each fiber scratching against his skin like needles. The lights overhead buzzed constantly, a sound no one else seemed to notice but felt deafening to him.

I could see the other children whispering, pointing at him. A boy approached and snatched his toy. The little boy let out a distressed sound, his hands flapping as he tried to express his anger and sadness, but the words wouldn't come.

The teacher intervened, scolding the other child, but the damage was done. The boy retreated further into himself, clutching his toy tighter. The world around him felt hostile, confusing, a place where he couldn't quite fit.

And then, in a sudden shift, the daycare melted away. I was standing in a small, cluttered apartment. Toys were scattered on the floor, some broken, others lovingly worn. There was the boy again, sitting cross-legged in the middle of the living room, his toy clutched to his chest. This time, the world around him was quieter, softer.

In the kitchen, I saw her—his mother. She was young, though the lines etched on her face made her seem older. Her dark hair was tied back in a messy ponytail, and she wore a wrinkled uniform, a name tag pinned to her chest. She moved with a weariness that spoke of long hours and too little rest, yet there was something unyielding in her every movement.

She glanced at her son and smiled though the weight of exhaustion hung heavy in her eyes. "How's my little superhero?" she asked, her voice warm despite her fatigue.

The boy didn't respond with words. Instead, he made a small sound—a hum, soft and almost musical. She didn't seem to mind. She knelt beside him, brushing a stray curl from his forehead. "You've had a big day, haven't you?" she said gently.

Her love for him was palpable. She worked tirelessly, juggling two jobs to keep a roof over their heads and food on the table. She knew his world was different, knew he faced challenges she couldn't always understand. But she loved him fiercely, unconditionally.

The apartment was simple and modest. The wallpaper peeled in places, and the furniture had seen better days. On the kitchen counter, a stack of bills sat next to an empty coffee mug. It was clear she was doing everything she could to make ends meet, to give her son the life he deserved. But no matter how hard her days were, she always found time for him.

I saw her sitting on the couch with him after dinner, reading to him even though he rarely made eye contact. Her voice was steady and warm as she brought the pages to life. The boy didn't respond, but I could see the way he held his toy a little tighter, the way his humming softened as if the story was seeping into his world.

Then when it was nighttime, the boy was lying in bed. His superhero toy was nestled beside him, his small hands resting protectively over it. His mother stood in the doorway, watching him with a tenderness that broke my heart. She leaned against the frame, her eyes filled with both love and worry.

"I'll always be here for you," she whispered, though he couldn't hear her. "You'll always be my little superhero."

Her words lingered in the air as the memory began to fade, pulling me back to the present. The boy's story, his struggles, his love for his toy—they all stayed with me, heavy and raw.

As I watched these moments unfold, I felt my heart ache for him. His life was filled with so much beauty—his mother's unwavering love, his own vivid imagination—but it was also marked by isolation, misunderstanding, and frustration. He lived in a world that didn't always have room for someone like him, a world that couldn't see how much he had to offer.

The moment I returned to the present, my fingers still lightly clutching the toy, a wave of understanding washed over me. I looked at the small, worn figure in my hand; its bright colors dulled from years of love and wear.

Now I knew why this toy was so important to him.

It wasn't just a toy—it was his connection to a world that often felt out of reach, a constant companion when words failed, a piece of safety and comfort in a life that could be overwhelming and unpredictable. It was more than plastic and paint; it was his lifeline.

By the time the ambulance had arrived, paramedics lifted Matthew's small, lifeless body onto a stretcher. His mother climbed into the ambulance with him, clutching his hand as if she could bring him back to life. The doors closed, and the siren wailed as they drove away.

The ghost of the boy stood beside me; his wide eyes fixed on the toy in my hand. Slowly, a faint smile spread across his pale lips. He didn't say any more words, but he smiled.

I stared at the spot where he had been, the toy clutched tightly in my hand. My chest felt heavy, a mix of sadness and relief washing over me. If I weren't there, he would've searched for his toy forever.

Later that night, I found out at work that Matthew did not make it. His mother came back that night to the hospital to pick up some of his clothes and to sign some papers.

I was on shift. I approached Matthew's mother, holding out the toy.

I sat in the quiet waiting area, my hands gently holding the boy's toy. The small action figure felt warm in my palm as though it carried a piece of him with it. I glanced at the boy's mother sitting across from me, her shoulders hunched as she wrung her hands nervously.

After a moment, I stood, walked over, and extended the toy toward her. "I think this belongs to your son," I said softly.

The mother looked up, startled. Her eyes, red and tired, flickered with recognition when she saw the toy. Her trembling hands reached for it, and as she held it to her chest, she let out a shaky breath.

"Thank you," she murmured, her voice barely above a whisper. She stared at the toy for a long moment, her fingers tracing its worn edges. "He used to love this one. Always kept it with him, no matter where we went."

I sat beside her, unsure of what to say but feeling the weight of something unspoken hanging in the air.

"He's non-verbal, you know," the mother said suddenly, her voice thick with emotion. "*He's never spoken a word. He was diagnosed with autism when he was just a toddler.*"

I listened but was surprised because I was sure he said a word asking me for his lost toy. My heart was aching as I sensed the depth of the woman's pain.

"It wasn't easy growing up," the mother continued, her words spilling out as though they'd been locked away for too long. "He was bullied so much. The world isn't kind to children who are different. But I was there—I tried to be. I learned to see the world the way he did, to understand what he needed, even when he couldn't say it."

She paused, her voice breaking. "I used to dream about hearing his voice. Just once. To hear him call me 'Mom.' I prayed for it every night. It became my only wish."

My fingers curled around the edge of her seat. I wanted to comfort her to say something meaningful, but I stayed quiet, letting her speak.

The mother let out a bitter laugh, her tears falling freely now. "But now I think... maybe I was wrong to wish for that. Maybe I didn't see how much he was already saying—without words. And now... now I'd give anything to go back. To hold him just as he was, to have him with me again. Silent or not, he was my boy."

Her sobs filled the quiet room as she clutched the toy to her chest. My throat tightened, the weight of the moment pressing against me.

"I just hope," the mother whispered, her voice trembling, "that he's found his voice wherever he is now. Maybe he's speaking all the things he couldn't say before."

I hesitated as I reached out to touch the woman's hand gently. "Maybe he has," I said softly but sure, "And maybe... maybe he's saying the things you always wanted to hear. That he loves you. That he's okay."

The mother looked at me with tears streaming down her face, a fragile smile breaking through the sorrow. "Do you think so?" she asked, her voice shaking.

"I do," I replied with my heart full of conviction. "Somewhere, in some way, maybe not in this lifetime, he found his voice."

The mother let out a shuddering breath with her grip on the toy loosening just slightly as the tension in her shoulders eased. "Thank you," she whispered; her words were barely audible but full of gratitude.

I sat with her in silence; the weight of the moment was pressing down on us like a tangible force. She held the toy close, her fingers trembling as if it were the last fragile connection to her son.

In his own little world of colors and shapes, this toy might have been his treasure, his anchor in a sea of the unfamiliar.

But to her, he was the most important thing—her entire world.

The love she poured into him, the patience she showed, and the countless nights she spent wishing for him to express the smallest of desires spoke of a bond far deeper than any words could ever convey.

For a moment, I thought the toy had been his most prized possession, the thing he clung to in his silent world. But as I watched her cradle the toy, I realized that I was wrong. It wasn't the toy itself that mattered most to him— it was her. He wanted her to have it, a piece of him to hold onto, a reminder of the love they shared and the moments they had. In that small gesture, he gave her the only way he could say, *I'll always be with you.*

And now, somehow, in a way I couldn't fully explain, *I felt certain he wasn't trapped in his own world anymore.* He was somewhere bigger, somewhere brighter. Somewhere, he had finally found his words. And in that moment, I could only hope that he was using it to tell her everything she'd longed to hear.

CHAPTER SEVEN: NIGHT SHIFT MADNESS

The hospital was unusually quiet tonight, a stark contrast to the usual commotion of an emergency room. The slight chatter created a soothing background noise—soft chatter, the occasional distant beep of a monitor, the shuffle of feet against the floor. You can smell freshly brewed coffee through the air, blending with the sterile, clean scent that always lingered in hospitals.

"Lila," Evelyn said, appearing beside me as I finished reviewing the day shift's handoff notes. Her voice was calm, almost motherly, and I didn't even startle for a second. "There's a patient waiting for you in Bay Three."

"Thanks," I said with a nod, setting my coffee down and grabbing the chart. But when I reached Bay Three, the bed was empty. The curtain hung still, and the monitor was off. Confused, I checked the chart again. Nothing was listed— no orders, no name.

I returned to the desk and scanned the patient board. No mention of Bay three there either. "Hey, did anyone discharge the patient in Bay three?" I asked Rowan, who was leaning against the counter.

Rowan furrowed her brows. "Bay three's been empty. Are you sure you didn't mix it up with Bay five?"

I shook my head. Maybe Evelyn had been mistaken. Or maybe it was the exhaustion setting in. I shrugged it off and busied myself with the rest of my patients.

#

Later than evening while I was restocking supplies in the storage room, Evelyn said something that I cannot stop on thinking.

"How are you adjusting, Lila?" she asked, her tone soft.

"I think I'm settling in," I said, arranging boxes of gloves on the shelf. "Everyone's been great, and the pace here is a lot less chaotic than what I'm used to."

Evelyn smiled faintly. "That's good to hear. But you should watch yourself around Dr. Pike."

I straightened up, caught off guard by her sudden shift in tone. "Why?"

She hesitated, as though weighing her words carefully. "Just... be careful."

I didn't get the chance to ask her what she meant, Evelyn seemed to be in a hurry and looked like she's been busy the whole night.

#

By the time I got a moment to breathe, it was already close to midnight. I leaned back in one of the rolling chairs at the desk and let out a long sigh. The team was settling into the rhythm of the shift. Maggie was swapping jokes with Luis, the two of them in hysterics over something too ridiculous to make sense out of context. Rowan, ever the voice of reason, was shaking her head at them, though she was clearly amused.

Rowan was finishing her charting nearby, and the easy banter between them was a welcome distraction.

Luis looked up and grinned at me. "You're settling in, huh?"

"I think so," I said, smiling. "It's a little quieter than what I'm used to, but I'm not complaining."

"Quieter?" Luis scoffed. "Just wait until flu season hits. Then you'll be begging for nights like this."

Maggie laughed. "And don't forget Dr. Pike's temper. That'll spice up your shift quickly."

I raised an eyebrow. "His temper?"

"Oh, you'll see," Maggie said, smirking. "He's quiet most of the time, but when he snaps, you'd better duck."

Luis leaned closer, his voice dropping to a conspiratorial tone. "Did Maggie tell you about the time he lost it on a patient? It was before you got here—a couple of months ago, maybe. This woman came into the ER having chest pain. She was fine. But halfway through her visit, she asked him if he was married."

"Why would she ask that?" I asked, confused.

Luis shrugged, grinning. "Who knows? Maybe she thought he was hot. Anyway, the question set him off. He yelled at her, right there in the middle of the ER. Told her she wasn't here to ask personal questions; she was here to get treated. It was... awkward, to say the least."

"Awkward?" Maggie said, laughing. "It was mortifying. The poor woman didn't say another word the rest of her visit."

Luis shook his head, still smiling. "So, yeah, if you catch him in a mood, tread lightly. He's a good doctor, but he's got his temper."

I filed the information away, thinking about Evelyn's earlier warning. *Be careful with him,* she'd said. Maybe there was more to Dr. Pike than I realized.

#

Around 2 a.m., I finished my rounds and decided to take a quick walk to wake myself up. The ER could get stifling after hours.

The hospital at night was a different world. The hallways were quiet, the soft glow of wall sconces casting long shadows. My footsteps echoed faintly as I wandered, passing the maternity ward on my way.

Something about the nursery window caught my eye. I paused, looking in at the row of cribs. Most were empty, but a few tiny bundles lay swaddled, their chests rising and falling with the rhythm of newborn sleep. The sight tugged at something deep in me, a quiet ache I couldn't quite name.

"Beautiful, isn't it?" Evelyn's voice broke the silence.

I turned to find her standing a few feet away, her gaze fixed on the nursery.

"It is," I said softly. "Hard to believe they'll grow up and end up in places like the ER someday."

Evelyn nodded, a small smile playing on her lips. "Life's funny that way. But even in the chaos, there's beauty. Don't forget that."

Her words lingered as she walked down the hallway, leaving me alone with my thoughts.

#

I'd been walking my usual route to stretch my legs and fight off the creeping drowsiness that always set in after 3 a.m. The coffee I'd guzzled earlier had done little to help.

Then, the overhead page woke me up: *"CODE BLUE, ED, BAY THREE. CODE BLUE, ED, BAY THREE."*

My heart jumped. Without a second thought, I broke into a sprint, my sneakers squeaking against the polished floor as I rounded the corner toward Bay 3. My pulse pounded in my ears, but as I approached, something felt... off.

When I arrived, the team was looking annoyed—Luis, Maggie, and Rowan—all standing in the empty bay with expressions that ranged from confusion to annoyance.

"Well," Luis said, gesturing toward the untouched bed, "who the hell pushed the button? There's no one here."

Rowan crossed her arms, frowning. "That's weird. I swear no one's been in this bay all night."

"Probably a malfunction," Maggie offered with a shrug. "Someone needs to call maintenance."

Luis nodded, running a hand through his hair. "Yeah, but seriously, this button's been acting up too much lately. It's going to give someone a heart attack. Bay three has been empty all night."

I glanced around, my chest still heaving from the run. It was the same bay Evelyn had directed me to earlier, where she'd said there was a patient waiting for me. And, just like then, there was no one here. My mind buzzed with questions, but I kept quiet.

"Well," Luis continued, clapping his hands together, "false alarm, folks. Back to your posts."

The others filed out, their chatter fading down the hall. I stayed, unable to shake the feeling that something wasn't right. The air in Bay Three felt different—colder, heavier. My breath misted slightly as I exhaled, a detail that made my stomach twist.

I stepped closer to the bed, scanning the area for any clue as to why the code blue button had been pressed. My fingers brushed the edge of the mattress, and the chill seemed to seep into my skin.

And then I felt it—*a familiar feeling. A tingling chill that runs all the way down to my feet.*

The cold intensified like a wave washing over me. I turned slowly, my hand trembling as I pulled back the curtain.

A man stood at the edge of the bed, his pale, lifeless face framed by neatly combed hair. He wore a tuxedo, slightly rumpled as if he'd been dancing in it all night. His lips were faintly blue, his skin waxy. His feet did not touch the floor.

I blinked hard, trying to steady my breath. He didn't move. Didn't speak. He just stood there; his hollow eyes fixed on me.

I closed my eyes, swallowing hard. *This isn't real,* I told myself. *You're just tired. You've been on edge all night.*

When I opened them again, he was gone.

I staggered back, pressing a hand to my chest as I tried to catch my breath. The chill remained like a shadow lingering in the corner of the room.

"Lila!"

I nearly jumped out of my skin at Luis's voice. He was leaning against the nurse's station while his brow furrowed.

"What day is it?" he asked, glancing at the wall clock.

I frowned, confused by the question. "Uh... October 12th? Why?"

Luis's face broke into a grin, though it didn't quite reach his eyes. "Hah! That explains it."

"Explains what?" I asked, my voice still shaky.

Luis stepped closer, glancing at the empty bed. "Bay 3, huh? Ten years ago today, we had a guy in here, his name is Charles—came in wearing a tuxedo, believe it or not. He was at some wedding reception and started having chest pain. We tried to get him to take it seriously, but he was a jokester, you know? Kept pressing the call button every five minutes, asking for water, or a snack, or just cracking some stupid joke."

I raised an eyebrow. "And?"

"And" Luis said, lowering his voice as if sharing a campfire ghost story, "he also pressed the code blue button. Twice. Just for laughs. By the time it got pressed again—

well, we thought it was another one of his jokes. But it wasn't."

I stared at him, the pieces clicking together in my mind.

"He died?" I whispered.

Luis nodded, his grin fading. "Yeah. Massive heart attack. When we finally got to him, it was too late. Couldn't bring him back. Poor guy was still in his tux. It was a real mess."

I felt the chill creep up my spine again, though I tried to play it off. "So... you think he's the one messing with the button?"

Luis chuckled, though there was an edge to it. "Hey, who knows? I wouldn't put it past him. He liked to mess with us when he was alive. Why stop now?"

I forced a laugh, but inside, my thoughts were spinning. *It couldn't be.*

Could it?

As Luis walked away, I stayed behind, staring at the empty bed. The air still felt heavy, and in the faintest corner of my mind, I thought I heard laughter—soft, raspy, and fading into the distance.

"Just a malfunction," I muttered to myself, turning to leave. But I couldn't shake the feeling that Bay three had more stories to tell.

CHAPTER EIGHT: THE PRANKSTER

I've been noticing things lately: small, almost insignificant oddities that only seem strange when you string them all together. For the past few weeks, charts have been mysteriously misplaced, only to turn up in places you'd never think to look. Pens go missing, only to roll off the counter hours later. My stethoscope has somehow ended up in the wrong pocket more than once. It's not just me, either—Luis swears his coffee cup disappeared one minute and reappeared the next, filled to the brim when he knows he drank it dry.

And then there are the call lights. Every shift, without fail, the call light in Bay Three goes off. Sometimes it's just once, other times it's three or four times in a row. Every time someone checks, the bay is empty. At first, it was funny—a harmless quirk of a malfunctioning button. But now, I'm not so sure.

Tonight, during a quiet moment in the nurses' station, Luis and Rowan were joking about it again.

"That call light in Bay Three," Luis said, shaking his head with a grin. "It's got to be the prankster ghost. He's been at it again."

"Prankster ghost?" I asked, raising an eyebrow.

Rowan leaned back in her chair, smirking. "Oh, yeah. Bay Three's got a reputation. The ghost loves messing with new staff. Steals pens, hides charts, that kind of thing."

Luis chimed in, "You know how it is—some patients never let go, even after they're gone."

I chuckled, but the idea stuck with me. If there was a spirit behind all these antics, I needed to know why. So later, while everyone else was on their lunch break, I decided to face him. Enough was enough.

I stood in front of Bay Three, the curtain drawn and the call light blinking mockingly. My pen, which had rolled off my desk earlier, was in my pocket, but I could swear it felt heavier than usual—like it was daring me to figure this out.

I took a deep breath and yanked the curtain open, ready to scold whatever lingering spirit was there.

That's when I saw him.

Sitting on the hospital bed was a man in his late forties, maybe early fifties. He wore a tux that seemed almost translucent, his pale skin glowing faintly under the overhead light. His hair was messy, his face tired, but he had a mischievous grin that somehow didn't reach his eyes.

"Are you... Charles?" I asked, remembering the name Luis had mentioned in passing.

His grin widened, and he gave a little bow. "At your service. And you must be Lila, the new nurse everyone's talking about."

I folded my arms, trying to steady my nerves. "Why are you doing this? The pens, the charts, the call lights—what do you want?"

Charles stood; his feet were not touching the floor. He moved closer, his hands outstretched. "I don't mean to be a bother," he said softly. "But maybe you're the only one who can help me."

Before I could ask what, he meant, his fingers brushed my arm. The room spun, the lights flickered, and suddenly, everything changed.

As I was pulled into Charles's memory, the world around me blurred and shifted. The cold, sterile walls of the hospital dissolved, and I found myself standing in a modest living room. The furniture was simple, worn with time, and the air felt heavy—not with anger, but with the quiet weight of sorrow and loneliness.

There, I saw a man sitting at a small wooden table. His eyes were tired, his hands calloused, resting on a stack of unopened letters. He wasn't the prankster everyone had whispered about. He was a man burdened by regret; misunderstood by the people he had loved the most.

I watched him leave his house each morning, his footsteps slow, his shoulders hunched. He looked as if he carried the weight of the world on his back. His job was demanding, and every long hour he worked seemed to chip away at him. But I could see it in his eyes—he left every day for them. For his family. To give them what he thought they needed.

But then, I saw the moments he couldn't give them. The birthdays he missed, the soccer games he wasn't there to cheer for, the graduation where his seat sat empty. I could feel the regret radiating from him, his eyes growing sadder with each memory. He had worked so hard for them, yet it had cost him the very moments that mattered most.

And then, I saw the day his wife and son left. It wasn't dramatic—no shouting, no slamming doors. Just bags quietly packed, tears on his wife's face as she stood in the doorway. "You were never here," she said, her voice trembling. "And what you did... it was never enough."

I could feel his heartbreak as they walked out the door. He didn't chase after them, didn't argue or plead. He just stood there, frozen, as his entire world slipped away.

The scene shifted, and I was back in that quiet house. But now it was emptier. He sat at the table again, those same letters in front of him, only now they were marked "Return to Sender." I watched him write to his son over and over, his handwriting shaky, the words filled with a father's love and desperation. Each letter sent, only to be returned unopened.

I saw him late at night, sitting by the phone, dialing his son's number. His hands shook as the phone rang and rang, but no one ever answered. Each unanswered call seemed to carve a deeper wound in his heart.

And then, the hardest thing to see: Charles standing outside his son's school, hiding behind a tree. He was clutching his coat like it could shield him from the reality of his life. I watched as he peeked out, just trying to catch a glimpse of his son. He didn't dare approach—too afraid of rejection, too broken to face the truth. But in that moment, I saw the longing in his eyes. He didn't just want to see his son—he wanted to undo everything, to go back and be the father his son needed.

I felt tears sting my own eyes as I stood there, an unseen witness to a life filled with so much love, so much sacrifice, and so much pain. Charles wasn't a bad man. He was a man who had tried—tried so hard—but in the end, it wasn't enough. He gave everything he had, but what he gave couldn't hold his family together.

And now, all that was left was this overwhelming regret. Letters unopened, phone calls unanswered, and the haunting image of a father standing in the shadows and stuck in a loop, watching a life he was no longer part of and relieving the night he passed. He wasn't just a ghost—he was a man searching for peace, for forgiveness, and for the love he had never stopped longing for.

Then his memory that I was in shifted back to the hospital. I was still in Bay Three, but it wasn't the same. The walls were a slightly different color, and the equipment was older. Luis walked past the bay, looking younger, his hair shorter and his face was less worn by years of night shifts. Juan, the janitor, was mopping the floor, his uniform crisp and clean. Two other nurses I didn't recognize were chatting by the station, their laughter echoing softly.

And there, sitting on the bed in Bay Three, was Charles. He looked alive, his cheeks flushed and his grin full of life. I watched as he pressed the call light again, then chuckled to himself when no one came immediately. He pressed the code blue button multiple times; everybody started running.

"Just wait," he muttered under his breath, clearly amused by his antics.

One of the nurses—tall, with dark hair tied in a bun— peeked into the bay and shook her head. "Charles, knock it off. We're not falling for it again."

He laughed, raising his hands in mock surrender. "All right, all right. I'll behave."

But the moment she left, he pressed the button again, this time was the code blue button laughing quietly to himself. Everybody ran to his bay,

I wanted to yell at him, to tell him to stop, but I couldn't move or speak. I was just an observer, trapped in his memory.

Then, his demeanor changed. His grin faded, and his brows furrowed as he pulled his phone from his pocket. The screen lit up, showing a name: **Michael**.

His hand trembled as he stared at the phone, his smile fading completely. "Michael..." he whispered, his voice almost reverent.

But before he could answer, he winced, clutching his chest. The phone slipped from his hand, clattering to the floor as he doubled over in pain. His breathing became labored, his face contorted in agony.

"Help," he gasped, reaching for code blue button. He pressed it while his fingers trembling.

This time, no one came. I saw the panic in his eyes as he realized they weren't going to take him seriously. He tried to call out, but his voice was too weak. His hand reached for the phone on the floor, but he couldn't make it. The last thing I saw was the look of regret on his face as he collapsed back onto the bed, the call light and code blue light still blinking.

I blinked, the memory dissolving around me as I returned to the present. Charles was standing in front of me again, his hands in his pockets, his expression heavy with regret.

"It was my son," he said quietly. "Michael. I wasn't a good dad; I was absent in many ways. My son never wanted to be around me. He never called me, not in years. But that night... he did. And I couldn't answer."

Tears welled in my eyes as I saw the pain etched on his face.

He looked at me, his voice trembling. "I just need to hear his voice. Just one word. One hello. That's all."

Back at the station, I pulled up Charles's old chart. His emergency contact was listed as Michael Warren, along with an address and phone number. My hands shook as I scribbled down the information.

I returned to Bay Three, holding my phone like it was a lifeline. Taking a deep breath, I dialed the number and put the call on speaker.

The phone rang twice before a man's voice answered. "Hello?"

I froze, the weight of the moment pressing down on me. Charles stood beside me; his gaze fixed on the phone.

"Hello?" the voice repeated, softer this time.

In the background, I heard the faint cry of a baby. "It's okay, it's okay, honey," Michael said, his tone warm and soothing while hushing. "I got you."

Charles's face lit up, his expression softening as a smile spread across his lips. He closed his eyes, his shoulders relaxing for the first time. The glow around him grew brighter, filling the room with a gentle warmth, knowing that his son was now grown and became the dad he never was.

"Thank you," his whisper echoed, his voice barely audible. "Thank you."

And then, just like that, he was gone.

The call disconnected, leaving me standing alone in Bay Three, the air heavy with silence. I held the phone to my chest, Charles was gone, but his smile, his peace, would stay with me forever.

I didn't know until now that one *hello* could give someone the closure they need and that one hello could also mean 'goodbye'.

CHAPTER NINE: FLESH AND BONES

The chatter echoed through the hospital corridors as I made my way toward the break room. The sound of the air conditioning accompanied the rhythmic beeping of the monitor. It was another quiet night shift—quiet, of course, by ER standards.

As I passed the ICU, the familiar chill of the hospital at night settled over me. The long hallway stretched ahead, dimly lit, casting elongated shadows along the walls. A flickering light caught my attention near the entrance to the Old Wing. I paused for a moment, curiosity tugging at me.

"What's in there?" I asked aloud, not really expecting an answer.

"You're always full of questions, aren't you?" Evelyn's voice startled me. She stood at the corner of the ICU, her arms crossed casually, her familiar half-smile teasing but warm.

"You scared me," I said, half-laughing as I caught my breath. "It feels like you're always working, Evelyn. When was the last time you took time off?"

She shrugged, looking almost wistful. "Work until you can't, I guess. Keeps the mind busy."

I studied her for a moment. Evelyn had a way of deflecting questions about herself, and tonight was no different. "Do you have family?" I asked.

For a brief second, her expression softened, something unreadable flashing in her eyes. "I have a daughter," she said simply. "But enough about me. You should get back to your break."

As she turned to leave, my gaze drifted back to the Old Wing. The flickering light and the darkness beyond seemed to whisper secrets I wasn't ready to uncover. Evelyn glanced back at me, as if sensing my curiosity.

"There are stories in this place," she said quietly. "But some of them aren't mine to tell. You'll have to find them for yourself."

Before I could respond, she was gone, her steps echoing faintly down the hallway. Evelyn is always busy.

I shook off the unease and continued toward the break room. That's when I saw her.

A small figure sat at the far end of the ICU, her frail body barely outlined in the shadows. Her sparse hair clung to her pale scalp, and her hollowed cheeks made her appear skeletal—more flesh and bone than a living being. Her gaze met mine, and for a moment, I froze.

"Excuse me, ma'am," I called out, stepping closer. But as I blinked, she was gone.

I felt my pulse quicken. I scanned the ICU, hoping someone else had seen her. The on-duty nurse, a middle-aged man with tired eyes, looked up from his charting as I approached.

The ICU felt like a world apart from the rest of the hospital. The sound of the ventilators and the IV pump beeping were the sounds you could hear through the night. The lights cast long shadows that seemed to stretch through the whole unit. I pretended I was just gathering supplies, but my curiosity about what I'd seen earlier was gnawing at me.

There she was again—the girl. Small, frail, and barely more than flesh and bones. Her hair was thin, her cheeks hollow, her skin so pale it seemed translucent. She was looking at me, but her eyes didn't meet mine; they seemed to look through me, as if searching for something—or someone.

As I pushed open the ICU doors, I scanned the rows of beds. It was quieter than usual. Most of the patients were unconscious, hooked up to machines keeping them tethered to life. I tried not to let the sterile stillness of the room get to me.

Feeling a sense of purpose, I approached the supply cart and started rifling through it, pretending to need something. My eyes darted toward the bed where I had seen the girl earlier. She wasn't standing there anymore, but the bed wasn't empty either.

The young woman lying in the bed was barely recognizable as human. Her limbs were so thin that her bones pressed sharply against her skin, her frame dwarfed by the tangle of tubes and wires surrounding her. Her chest rose and fell in shallow, uneven breaths, aided by the ventilator. Her hospital gown hung loosely on her skeletal frame, and the IV drips beside her bed pumped a steady stream of nutrients into her frail body.

"She's only fifteen," came a voice beside me. I turned to see an ICU nurse, standing with his arms crossed. "Sad, isn't it?"

"What happened to her?" I asked softly, unable to tear my eyes away from the girl.

The nurse sighed, his gaze heavy with something I couldn't quite place—empathy, exhaustion, maybe both. "Eating disorder. Starved herself to death, almost. She's been here for weeks, but... there's not much left of her. Her heart's giving out. All the organs are shutting down."

I felt a lump forming in my throat. "She's just a kid."

"Yeah," the nurse said, glancing at the monitors beside her bed. "She was a cheerleader, popular, they said. But... she was obsessed with her image. Too obsessed. It started with skipping meals, then purging, then refusing to eat altogether. Her mom brought her in when she collapsed at home. It was already too late by then."

The weight of his words pressed down on me. I didn't know this girl—didn't know her story beyond what the nurse had told me—but I felt the sting of loss all the same. I glanced back at her, at the way her sunken eyes barely flickered beneath her closed lids and wondered what had driven her to this point. What had made her feel like she wasn't enough?

The nurse's voice broke through my thoughts. "Her mom's devastated. She's been here every day, but we had to send her home to rest. She blames herself, but there's nothing she could've done. Sometimes... it's not anyone's fault."

I nodded mutely, my chest tight. The girl in the bed looked so small, so fragile. And yet, there was a strength in her presence, a story she seemed to carry even in silence.

As the nurse stepped away to check on another patient, I felt a chill pass over me. It wasn't the cold, clinical air of the ICU—it was something else. I turned back to the girl's bed and saw her, standing just beside her own body. Her ghostly figure mirrored her frail form, but her eyes were wide open now, filled with a mixture of sorrow and defiance.

I froze, my heart was pounding in my chest. She looked at me, really looked at me this time, and I felt an unspoken plea in her gaze. I couldn't move. I couldn't speak. All I could do was stand there, locked in the weight of her unspoken words.

The nurse's voice broke through the haze. "Hey, you, okay?" he asked, glancing at me curiously.

"Yeah," I said quickly, trying to shake off the lingering chill. "Just... tired, I guess."

He nodded sympathetically as he goes back to the nurse's station. "Night shift does that to you. Hang in there."

I managed a weak smile and returned to the supply cart, but my mind spun. The girl's presence had been so vivid, so real. And the look in her eyes—it wasn't just sadness. It was regret.

Evelyn's words from earlier echoed in my mind: *"It's for you to find out.*

I didn't know what Evelyn meant yet, but I had a feeling I was about to find out.

As I stepped closer to the patient on the bed, a faint whisper brushed against my ear, soft yet chilling as if carried on a ghostly breeze: *"Help... I am starving."*

My breath hitched, and my feet felt cemented to the floor. The words echoed in my mind, impossible to ignore. Trembling, I reached out, hesitant but compelled. As my fingers grazed her fragile arm, the world around me seemed to blur and dissolve. A new reality unfolded before me, vivid and haunting.

There she was—a teenage girl with radiant energy, her cheerleading uniform bright and spotless, her hair tied perfectly with ribbons that danced in the wind. Her laugh rang out as she practiced routines with her teammates, her movements graceful and precise. She exuded confidence, the kind of girl who naturally drew people's attention, the one everyone wanted to be around. Her team cheered her on, and she waved to a group of friends watching from the sidelines.

But then, as the scene shifted slightly, I noticed something else. Beyond the lively persona was a girl tethered to her phone. She sat on her bed, scrolling through her social media feed, her smile lighting up her face as likes and comments poured in.

"You're so gorgeous!"

"Slay, queen!"

"Cheer captain vibes!"

Her grin widened, her heart soaring with the dopamine rush. It was intoxicating, the kind of validation she craved. But as she continued scrolling, her expression faltered.

"She looks bigger this year. Is she pregnant?"

The comment was cruel and biting, standing out like a jagged thorn amidst a bed of roses. She read it once, twice, and then a third time, her hands tightening around the phone. Her breathing quickened, and she clutched her stomach reflexively. The bright glow of the screen seemed to dim, its light now casting shadows across her face.

The scene shifted again. She was standing in front of her mirror, her cheerleading uniform hugging her frame as she twisted and turned, scrutinizing every angle. Her hands tugged at the fabric, pulling it tighter as if willing herself to shrink. Her reflection stared back, cruel and judgmental.

Her fingers skimmed over her ribs, her shoulders shaking as silent tears streamed down her cheeks. She whispered to herself, words I could barely hear but knew all too well: *"I'm not enough. I'll never be enough."*

The mirror became her battlefield. Each day, she stood there, dissecting her reflection, hunting for flaws. The vibrant, lively girl I had seen moments earlier was slowly fading, replaced by someone desperate for control, for perfection.

I saw her at the dinner table, her family gathered around her. Her plate sat untouched as she pushed the food around with her fork, offering weak excuses. *"I ate earlier. I'm just not hungry right now."* Her mother's worried glance went unnoticed as the girl kept her gaze fixed downward.

Back in her room, I saw her meticulously planning her meals—or lack thereof. Water, an apple slice, maybe a cracker. Then I saw her going to the bathroom bringing her finger at the back of her throat, gagging and retching until her knees buckled.

Her social media feed became a haven of harmful hashtags and accounts promoting impossible standards. She smiled when the scale's number dropped but cried alone when the hollowness inside her grew.

The scenes unraveled quickly now, each one sharper and more heartbreaking than the last. I saw her at school, her movements sluggish, her once-vibrant energy drained. I saw her friends whispering, their eyes darting toward her shrinking frame. And yet, she kept smiling, determined to show the world she was fine.

Her cheerleading uniform hung off her body like a shadow of its former self. Her teammates screamed, rushing to her side as she hit the floor. Paramedics arrived, their faces tense as they worked quickly to stabilize her. But even then, even in her weakest moment, she whispered, *"I'm fine. I don't need help."*

As I stood there, the whisper from earlier lingered in my ears: *"Help me... I'm starving."* But now I understood—it wasn't food she was craving. It was something deeper, something far more complex. She was starving for approval, for validation, for the kind of love that didn't come from the glow of a screen but from the people who truly mattered.

I was pulled back into her memory, and this time, I saw her sitting on the edge of her bed, her knees pulled up to her chest. Her phone was clutched tightly in her hand, its screen dimmed, her social media feed paused on that cruel comment. Her shoulders shook as she let out a soft, muffled sob.

In the reflection of the mirror across from her, I saw her gaze shift—not to herself, but to a family photo on her nightstand. It was a picture of her younger self, grinning broadly, her arms wrapped around her parents. Her mother's hand rested protectively on her shoulder; her father's arm draped casually over her other side. They looked happy, carefree. The girl in that photo radiated joy.

But now, as she sat there staring at the picture, her expression hardened. I could feel the weight of her thoughts as though they were my own: *"Why can't I be that girl again? Why can't I be the girl they're proud of?"*

Her phone slipped from her hand and landed with a soft thud on the floor. She stared blankly at the family photo, her lips trembling as tears rolled down her cheeks.

"You're not enough." The words weren't coming from the outside anymore. They were etched into her mind, playing on repeat. And yet, underneath all that pain, there was a quiet, desperate hope.

She wasn't waiting for the world's approval. She wasn't waiting for the likes or the comments to validate her existence. The only opinion that truly mattered was her parents'. The approval she sought wasn't from strangers—it was from them.

In the stillness of her room, I could feel the tension she carried, the yearning for her mother to tell her she was beautiful as she was, for her father to say she was perfect just the way she'd always been. Her need for their reassurance was palpable, a silent scream that went unanswered.

Her gaze lingered on the photo as though willing the younger version of herself to speak, to remind her parents who she used to be, to make them see her again. But the silence in her room was deafening, her cries buried under the weight of their busy lives and her own mounting despair.

Now I understood. Her whispers weren't just about food—they were about love. About belonging. About being seen and being enough for the people she loved the most. Tears welled in my own eyes as I stood there, the heavy truth settling into my chest.

She wasn't just starving her body—she was starving her soul, longing for words from her parents that could have filled the void within her. Words that could have reminded her she didn't need to be anything but herself. But those words never came, and the weight of their absence consumed her.

I stood there frozen, my heart heavy as her mother walked into the room. She looked exhausted, her eyes red-rimmed and tired, carrying the weight of something too immense to put into words. Her steps faltered as she approached the frail, motionless body in the bed, and her voice broke as she spoke to me.

"She was so full of life," her mother whispered, tears streaming down her face. "She loved to dance. Cheerleading competitions, recitals—she was always on the move. But…" Her voice caught, and she struggled to continue. "We were always at work. Her father and I—we missed so much. I missed her competitions, her recitals… everything. I didn't see what was happening."

Her words pierced through the room like a lament too late to be heard. I glanced at the girl, who now stood next to her own frail body. She looked at her mother with hollow eyes, her skeletal frame a haunting reminder of what was lost. She said nothing, but the pain in her gaze spoke volumes.

I swallowed hard, my voice trembling as I spoke. "You can still talk to her, you know. Hearing is the last sense to go. Even if it feels like she can't hear you, she might. Sometimes, it's the words we never say that matter most."

Her mother's shoulders shook as she sat down beside the bed. She reached out, her trembling hand brushing the girl's bony fingers. She began to sob, whispering through her tears, "I'm so sorry. I'm sorry we weren't there enough. I'm sorry we didn't see. We should have known…"

The girl didn't move, but her ghostly form shifted closer as though drawn to her mother's words.

Her mother continued, her voice thick with emotion. "We were always so busy, caught up in work, trying to give you a better life. But we missed what really mattered—you. You were enough. You were always enough, sweetheart. We didn't tell you enough, but you were perfect to us."

At those words, something shifted in the room. The air felt lighter, almost warm. The girl's ghost, still frail and skeletal, straightened slightly. Her sunken eyes filled with something that hadn't been there before—peace. She didn't speak, but her gaze softened as she looked at her mother.

Her mother wept openly now, leaning over to press her forehead to her daughter's hand. "We should have told you more. I should have told you more. I hope you can forgive us."

The girl's ghost looked at me one last time, her hollow cheeks lifting into the faintest of smiles. She gently touched her mother's shoulder, though her mother couldn't feel it.

The sound of the heart monitor suddenly flatlined. The piercing tone filled the room, sharp and final, cutting through the air like a blade. In seconds, the ICU sprang to life. Nurses and doctors rushed in, the sound of hurried footsteps and sharp commands filling the small space.

But even amidst the flurry of activity, I knew it was too late. The girl's frail, skeletal body on the ventilator couldn't fight anymore. Her spirit, standing just a few feet away, watched quietly, detached from the chaos as though she had already made peace with what was happening.

Finally, after what felt like an eternity, the lead doctor stood back, his gloves stained with effort. His voice was calm but heavy, each word landing with a terrible finality.

"Time of death: 2:47 a.m."

Then, with a slow, fading glow, her ghost began to dissipate, leaving the air shimmering faintly in her wake.

Sometimes, in the world full of different opinions and voices, words of the people we love are the only words that matter.

And in that moment, I knew the girl had finally found peace.

Her mother didn't notice, lost in her grief. But I saw it. *I saw the glow she left behind, a small, quiet warmth that lingered even after she was gone.*

CHAPTER TEN: THE OLD WING

I walked back into the chaos of the ER. It was flu season, and RSV cases were through the roof. The bays were packed with coughing children, exhausted parents, and a steady stream of ambulance arrivals. Luis had caught the bug, leaving Rowan and me to hold down the fort alongside Dustin, a float nurse from the ICU.

"Great," I muttered under my breath as I tied my hair back. "Short-staffed on the busiest night of the season."

"Welcome to the trenches," Rowan said with a wry smile as we passed each other at the station.

I grabbed a chart and headed toward one of the bays. The patient inside—a middle-aged woman with a headache—

looked uneasy. I introduced myself and began the assessment.

"Need a hand?" Evelyn's calm voice broke through the noise.

I turned to see her standing at the edge of the bay, clipboard in hand. Relief washed over me. "Thank God you're here. It's a madhouse tonight."

Evelyn offered a small smile but said nothing more. As I continued to check the patient, her condition suddenly deteriorated. Her body stiffened, and her eyes rolled back as she began seizing. I froze, my mind going blank as panic set in.

"Lila!" Evelyn's voice was sharp but steady. "Get the suction. Now."

I snapped out of it, grabbing the suction and positioning the patient. "Turn her on her side," Evelyn instructed. "Keep her airway clear."

With Evelyn's guidance, I managed to stabilize the patient until the seizure stopped. My heart raced, but relief settled in as the patient's breathing evened out.

"Thank you," I whispered to Evelyn, shaken but grateful.

She placed a hand on my shoulder, her touch grounding. "You did great. Remember, it's all about staying calm."

Evelyn had saved me more times than I could count. I remember one instance vividly—a patient wasn't responding, and before I even stepped into the bay, Evelyn was already shouting for me to grab the crash cart. Her instincts were razor-sharp, the kind that only comes from years of experience. She reminded me of my stepmom in so many ways—seasoned, calm, and endlessly caring. Evelyn had a way of making me feel safe, even in the middle of chaos. She always put the patients first, never hesitating to stay late or go the extra mile, no matter how exhausted she must have been. Her dedication was unmatched, and I couldn't help but admire her for it.

The rest of the night was a blur of patients and chaos. By the time the shift ended, I felt like I'd run a marathon. As I gathered my things to leave, I spotted Evelyn walking toward the Old Wing. The dimly lit corridor looked even more foreboding than usual.

I was about to step closer to the doors of the old wing when I heard a voice behind me, firm but calm.

"Lila," Dr. Pike called out.

I froze and turned around slowly, feeling my heart pound as though I'd been caught doing something I shouldn't. He stood a few feet away, his hands in his coat pockets, his expression unreadable.

"Heading somewhere?" he asked, his tone polite but edged with curiosity.

"I—uh, no, not really," I stammered, suddenly feeling the weight of his gaze. "I was just... stretching my legs before heading out."

Dr. Pike raised an eyebrow, glancing toward the old wing. "Stretching your legs all the way to the most prohibited area of the hospital?"

I swallowed hard, feeling the heat rise to my cheeks. "I didn't realize I was that close. I guess I got turned around."

He nodded, but his eyes lingered on me for a moment too long. "The old wing is off-limits for a reason. It's not safe. The fire damage left it unstable, and frankly, it's better left alone."

"I understand," I replied quickly, hoping to sound more convincing than I felt. "I wasn't planning to go in or anything."

Dr. Pike took a step closer, his expression softening slightly. "You're curious, aren't you? Go home Lila." he asked, though it sounded more like an observation than a question.

I walked away from the old wing, but it stayed in my mind. The image of Evelyn going into the old wing but was it really Evelyn that I saw?

I was off for a couple of days after that shift, and I used the time to explore Nightfall Pines. I wandered through the town's streets, stopping at shops and savoring the time off I have. At Thai Tasty, I ordered the spiciest dish on the menu, laughing through watery eyes as the heat overwhelmed my senses. It was a brief respite from the chaos of work.

When I returned to the hospital, Luis was back, looking pale but determined to power through his shift.

"Miss me?" he asked, grinning as he pulled on his gloves.

"Like a hole in the head," I joked, relieved to see him.

Later that night, Luis was at the nurses' station, engrossed in something on his tablet. Rowan was across from him, updating a patient chart. I slid into a chair next to Luis, holding my cup of coffee like a lifeline.

"What's got you so serious tonight?" I asked, trying to sound casual, though my real agenda was brewing in the back of my mind.

"Trying to figure out when we can send some patients to the floor," he said without looking up. "Why? You look like you've got something on your mind."

I hesitated, choosing my words carefully. "Just... curious about the Old Wing. What's the story with that place?"

Luis glanced up, his expression shifting from curious to mischievous. "Oh, so you've been drawn to the infamous Old Wing, huh? You're not the first."

Rowan looked up from her chart and smirked. "Let me guess, you passed by, and the flickering lights got to you?"

"Something like that," I said, shrugging. "It just... feels off. Like it's watching you."

Luis chuckled. "That sounds about right. The Old Wing has its fair share of stories. Want the long version or the short one?"

"Give me the long one," I said, leaning in.

Luis leaned back, his arms crossed, clearly relishing the moment. "Alright. So, fifty years ago, the Old Wing wasn't 'old.' It was just another part of the hospital. Then there was a fire. Big one. Rumor has it that one of the patients was smoking while on oxygen. You can guess what happened next. The patient exploded and created fire throughout the wing."

I nodded, sipping my coffee to mask the unease creeping up my spine.

"The fire spread fast," Luis continued. "They evacuated as many patients as they could, but the weird thing is... nobody died in the worst-hit area except for the patient who created the fire"

"How's that possible?" I asked, my voice steady but my heart pounding.

"That's the mystery," Luis said, his tone dropping for dramatic effect. "The patients claimed they were saved by a nurse. A woman. But here's the thing: no female nurses were working that night in that section. Just two male nurses, Eddie and Sam. Eddie got burned badly, but he survived. Sam was hospitalized for weeks."

I frowned, the story raising more questions than answers. "So, who was she?"

Luis shrugged. "No one knows. Some say it was an angel. Others think it was a spirit or something. The patients swore she was real, though. They even described her—dark hair, kind eyes, calm voice."

Rowan chimed in, "And she just disappeared after the fire. Like, vanished. No one ever figured out who she was."

I glanced toward the direction of the Old Wing, the weight of their words settling on my chest. "That's... strange."

Luis nodded. "That whole place is strange. They shut it down after the fire, but people still say they hear things coming from there. Footsteps, whispers, stuff like that. They're saying that since it is abandoned, spirits might have found their place to hang out."

Rowan grinned. "You're not planning on going in there, are you?"

"Of course not," I lied, my curiosity burning brighter with every word.

CHAPTER ELEVEN: BEYOND DEATH

My eyes scanned each corner, each nurse's station, searching for a familiar figure. But Evelyn was nowhere to be found.

"Hey, Luis," I began, leaning against the counter. "Have you seen Evelyn tonight? Is she off?"

Luis looked up at me, his brows furrowing slightly. "Evelyn?"

I tilted my head at him. "Yeah, Evelyn. The Nurse Supervisor."

Luis blinked at me, his expression blank. "Lila, I have no idea who you're talking about."

"What do you mean, 'who'? Evelyn. She's always around. She's been here every shift I've worked," I said, laughing nervously. "You're playing with me, right?"

Luis shook his head slowly, setting down his pen. "Lila, I've worked here for over ten years. We don't have a nurse supervisor on night shift. This is a small hospital. We don't even have the budget for that kind of position."

I felt the blood drain from my face. "But—last night, I saw her," I insisted. "She walked into the old wing."

"The old wing?" Luis repeated, his voice dropping slightly. "Lila, you know that area is off-limits. No one goes in there. It's been closed for decades."

"No," I said, shaking my head. "She was there. I saw her. You're telling me she doesn't work here? That she doesn't exist?"

Luis leaned forward; concern etched on his face. "Lila, I'm telling you, there's no Evelyn here. Maybe you're just overtired. It's been a crazy week. You should take a break."

I nodded slowly, though my mind was racing. "Yeah... maybe you're right. Can you cover me for a bit?"

"Of course," Luis said, giving me a reassuring smile. "Take your time."

I walked away from the station, my heart pounding in my chest. My hands trembled slightly as I made my way down the hall. The pieces of the puzzle weren't fitting, and the more I tried to make sense of it, the more disoriented I felt.

As I walked down the quiet hallway, my steps slowed, and a wave of unease settled over me. My mind raced, replaying every interaction I'd ever had with Evelyn. The way she always seemed to appear at just the right moment, guiding me through chaotic shifts, her calm demeanor steadying me like an anchor. She was more than just a coworker—she felt like a mentor, almost motherly in how she cared.

Evelyn didn't exist? How could that be possible? I'd spoken to her. She'd helped me. She'd been as real to me as anyone else on the floor. She'd touch my shoulder. I knew it was real.

The image of her disappearing into the old wing flashed in my mind. Standing in front of the dimly lit hallway that led to the sealed doors, I stopped walking. The old wing.

A chill ran down my spine as I stared at the flickering light above the entrance. I had been told not to go there. Dr. Pike's warning replayed in my head, but curiosity gnawed at me, louder and more insistent than any caution.

Before I could talk myself out of it, I started down the hallway. Each step echoed, the sound magnified in the emptiness. My breathing was shallow, and my pulse thundered in my ears. Whatever was happening, whatever Evelyn was, I needed answers.

When I reached the sealed doors of the old wing, I hesitated. The air felt colder here, heavier, as though the past clung to the walls. With a deep breath, I placed my hand on the door handle. It felt ice-cold beneath my fingers.

I pulled it open.

The temperature seemed to drop instantly, the air felt heavy like a brick. It smelled of age—stale and musty, like old books forgotten in a damp attic. But beneath that, there was something else. A faint, burnt scent lingered in the air, one I couldn't quite place. Burnt wood? Smoke? It was faint but unmistakable.

The lights above me flickered sporadically, casting uneven shadows across the hallway. The walls were lined with faded, peeling paint, and patches of discoloration hinted at water damage from years past. I instinctively wrapped my arms around myself as I walked further in, my footsteps echoing faintly in the eerie silence. The floor beneath me creaked, each sound amplified in the emptiness.

Old photographs hung askew on the walls, their glass cracked or missing entirely. I paused in front of one—a black-and-white image of nurses gathered around a patient. The edges of the photo were charred, as though it had been salvaged from a fire. Their faces were blurry, but their uniforms reminded me of a time long before mine. A wave of unease washed over me. How long had these been here? And why had no one removed them?

Further down the hall, I saw an old stretcher propped against the wall, its metal frame rusted, and its fabric torn. I hesitated, brushing my fingers lightly over the edge of it, and the metal felt unnervingly cold under my touch. Next to it, a long-forgotten IV pole stood at an awkward angle, its wheels caked with grime as though it hadn't been moved in decades.

As I continued walking, I passed what appeared to be an old office. The door was ajar, and I peered inside. The room was small, cluttered with dusty papers and a desk that looked ready to collapse under their weight. An ancient typewriter sat in the center; its keys covered in cobwebs.

The sight was haunting, as though the room had been abandoned mid-shift, frozen in time.

The further I ventured, the heavier the air felt, pressing against my chest like an invisible weight. My heart raced, the pulse in my ears competing with the sound of my shoes on the worn linoleum. I tried to steady my breathing, but every step felt harder than the last.

Old medical equipment was scattered throughout the hallway—wheelchairs with broken spokes, oxygen tanks long since emptied, and surgical trays with instruments still resting on them, dulled by time. Everything looked as though it had been left in a hurry, and I couldn't shake the feeling that the walls themselves held memories of the chaos that once consumed this place.

The flickering light cast a shadow on an old bulletin board, where faded notes and memos clung stubbornly to their tacks. One caught my eye—a handwritten schedule for staff, dated over 50 years ago. The names were barely legible, but I couldn't help but scan them, looking for something familiar.

I turned a corner and stopped abruptly. A wheelchair was sitting in the middle of the hallway, facing me as though waiting. My breath caught in my throat as I stared at it, my mind racing. Had it always been there? I hadn't noticed it before. The hallway stretched into darkness beyond it, and for a moment, I felt paralyzed, unable to move forward.

A chill ran through me as I heard a faint creak behind me. I spun around, heart pounding, but there was nothing. Just the empty hallway I had walked through moments ago. The silence was deafening, broken only by the faint sound of the lights blinking nonstop.

I took a shaky step forward, then another, edging closer to the wheelchair. The wheels were covered in dust, but the seat looked oddly clean, as though it had been used recently. I swallowed hard, forcing myself to move past it. My hands trembled as I wiped them on my scrubs, trying to calm the mounting panic rising in my chest.

Ahead, I noticed a door slightly ajar. It looked like it led to a larger room. My curiosity pulled me toward it, even as every instinct told me to turn back. As I approached, the faint sound of whispers reached my ears. They were too soft to make out but sent goosebumps racing across my skin. I paused, gripping the edge of the door, and took a deep breath before pushing it open.

What lay beyond was a large room filled with rows of empty hospital beds. Most were rusted, their mattresses torn or missing entirely. The room felt colder than the hallway, and the whispers seemed to vanish as soon as I stepped inside. The walls were adorned with more photos, some burned so badly that only fragments remained.

I walked to the center of the room, turning slowly to take it all in. It was unsettling; this space that once held life was now frozen in decay. I felt like I didn't belong here like I was trespassing on something sacred. My heart pounded as I turned to leave, but my feet felt heavy, rooted to the spot.

As my eyes scanned the walls of the room, they landed on another old photograph hanging crookedly among the others. It caught my attention immediately—not because it was clearer than the others, but because of the familiar face in the center of it. My breath hitched.

Evelyn.

The picture looked old and showed unmistakably Evelyn. Her smile was wide and radiant, her dark hair pulled back neatly into a bun. She stood proudly among a group of nurses, their crisp uniforms stark white against the faded backdrop of an older version of Nightfall Pines Hospital. The photo was dated at the bottom: *September 20, 1975.*

I took a step closer, my fingers trembling as I reached out to touch the glass covering the photograph. It was real. She was real. A wave of relief washed over me, though it was quickly tempered by confusion. How could this be possible? Evelyn looked exactly the same in this decades-old picture as she did now. The same beaming smile, the same warm eyes. My mind struggled to process it. Was I losing it? No, I couldn't be. This photograph was proof.

The sudden sound of a soft sound pulled me out of my thoughts; sounded like humming. It was faint, almost too faint to hear, but it carried a haunting and familiar melody. My heart pounded as I turned toward the direction it came from, the sound seeming to echo through the walls.

It was Evelyn.

I didn't hesitate. I followed the hum, my steps quickening as it grew louder. The melody wound its way through the empty halls, leading me deeper into the old wing. The air grew colder, the scent of smoke and ash heavier with each step. My heart raced as I turned corner after corner, the hum always just out of reach.

Finally, it led me to a door. It was heavy and rusted, with a small plaque that read *Boiler Room*. The hum stopped abruptly, and an eerie silence took its place. My hand hovered over the handle, hesitating for just a moment before I pushed it open.

The room beyond was dimly lit, the only light coming from an old, flickering bulb hanging from the ceiling. Pipes crisscrossed the walls, and the air was damp and thick with the scent of rust and oil. In the center of the room stood Evelyn.

She was facing away from me, her posture relaxed as though she had been expecting me. Her hands were clasped behind her back, and she was humming softly again, the same haunting melody that had guided me here. The sound sent a chill down my spine, and for a moment, I thought about turning back. But then she spoke.

"You found me, Lila."

Her voice was calm, almost cheerful, but it sent a jolt through me. How did she know I was looking for her? My throat felt dry, and I swallowed hard before finding my voice. "Evelyn... what are you doing here? This place... it's off-limits."

She turned to face me slowly, her expression warm but unreadable. "I could ask you the same thing," she said, tilting her head slightly. "Why did you follow me?"

"I..." I faltered, unsure of what to say. "I was just... worried. I saw you come down here one night, and I thought..." My voice trailed off, the words feeling inadequate. "I thought you might need help."

Evelyn smiled faintly, the kind of smile that seemed to hold a thousand secrets. "You're kind, Lila. Always looking out for others." She took a step closer, her eyes locking onto mine.

Her words sent a chill through me, though I couldn't quite explain why. "Evelyn... what are you talking about? What is happening?"

She didn't answer. Instead, she looked around the room, her gaze softening as though she was lost in her own memories. "This hospital has seen so much, Lila. So many lives were saved, and so many were lost. Each one leaves something behind... echoes, if you will."

"Echoes?" I repeated my voice barely above a whisper.

Evelyn nodded. "Memories, feelings, fragments of who they were. They linger, waiting for someone to notice, to remember. That's why I'm here, Lila.

She gave me a sad smile, one that didn't quite reach her eyes. "Lila, the ones who stay behind are the ones who can't let go."

Her words hit me like a punch to the gut, and I couldn't breathe for a moment.

I hesitated, every instinct screaming to demand answers. But something in her expression stopped me.

Without thinking, I reached out and gently touched Evelyn's arm. The moment my fingers brushed against her, the world around me shifted.

It was as if I had been plunged underwater, my breath catching as a wave of memories washed over me. The dim maintenance room disappeared, replaced by a bustling hospital ward, bright with activity. The air smelled like fresh flowers, and the sound of conversation filled the space. Nurses in crisp white uniforms moved with purpose, their shoes tapping rhythmically against the polished floor.

There, in the middle of it all, was Evelyn.

She was young, her face radiant with a kind of hope and energy that seemed to ripple through the air. Her smile was infectious, lighting up every room she entered. She moved gracefully between patients. She offered kind words to a man confined to his bed and gently stroked the hand of an elderly woman as she adjusted the IV line.

Evelyn shone the brightest. She was in her element here, a force of nature among the chaos. Every step she took was purposeful, every movement filled with grace. Her voice was soft yet steady, carrying an authority that calmed even the most anxious patients.

I watched her sit beside an elderly man who was visibly frightened about an upcoming procedure. She didn't rush him or offer empty reassurances. Instead, she took his hand in hers, her other hand resting gently on his shoulder.

"Mr. Callahan," she said softly, her eyes meeting his with unwavering kindness. "I know it's scary, but I promise I'll be with you every step of the way. We'll get through this together."

The man's trembling stopped as he looked into her eyes, as though her very presence was enough to steady him.

With another patient, a young boy with a broken arm, she crouched down to his level, her smile warm and inviting. "That cast is going to make you look so cool," she said, tapping the plaster lightly. "You'll be the bravest kid in school."

The boy sniffled, his tears subsiding as he stared at her in awe. "Really?" he asked, his voice small.

"Really," she replied with a wink. "And you can even get everyone to sign it. By the end of the week, it'll be a work of art."

Her care extended far beyond her medical duties. She noticed the small things others might overlook—a patient struggling with their blanket, someone too shy to ask for help reaching their water, a colleague who looked like they needed a moment to breathe. Evelyn was there for them all.

In one memory, a colleague frantically flipped through a chart, overwhelmed by the demands of the day. Evelyn placed a calming hand on their shoulder. "Take a deep breath," she said gently. "We'll handle this together."

She wasn't just a nurse; she was a lifeline. Her patience never wavered, even when faced with the most difficult patients or the longest shifts. When a patient was angry or frustrated, she listened without judgment, her calm presence diffusing the tension.

Evelyn worked tirelessly, often staying late to ensure everything was done properly. She had a way of making each patient feel like they were her only priority, giving them her full attention as though nothing else in the world mattered at that moment.

I couldn't help but marvel at her warmth. She turned briefly, rubbing her belly, and I realized she was pregnant. There was a glow about her, a happiness that radiated from within. Nurses passing by congratulated her, and she laughed, cradling her growing belly as if already bonding with the life inside.

But the scene shifted suddenly, jarringly.

I was pulled in her memory at home. The cheerful nurse was gone, replaced by a woman whose sad eyes told a different story. Her hands trembled as she stood by the sink, her shoulders hunched as though bracing for a storm. I watched as she glanced nervously at the clock and then at the door, her fear palpable.

The door opened, and a man stepped in. My heart clenched when I saw who it was—Dr. Pike. But younger. Dr. Pike was Evelyn's husband.

"What are you doing standing there like that?" His voice was sharp, cutting through the air like a blade.

"I was just—" Evelyn started, but before she could finish, his hand lashed out, slapping her across the face. The sound echoed in the room, freezing me in place. She stumbled backward, hitting the wall with a thud, cradling her belly instinctively. Tears streamed down her face as she whispered something I couldn't hear.

After that, Evelyn sat on the edge of the bed, holding a compact mirror in one hand and a makeup brush in the other. She dabbed carefully at the bruises on her cheek and the cut on her lip, her face a mask of concentration.

Her reflection in the mirror revealed more than just her physical injuries—it showed the exhaustion in her eyes, the way they seemed to hold back a torrent of unspoken words, unexpressed pain. She dabbed more powder on her cheek, tilting her head to ensure the bruise was fully covered. When she was done, she snapped the compact shut and took a deep breath, squaring her shoulders as if putting on armor.

In another moment, I saw her sitting at the dinner table, nervously twirling her fork as Dr. Pike sat across from her, ranting about something insignificant. She nodded quietly, her lips pressed into a thin line, her eyes fixed on the table.

"You could at least pretend to be listening," he snapped, slamming his hand down on the table, making the silverware rattle. Evelyn flinched, her fork clattering onto her plate.

"I'm sorry," she murmured, her voice barely audible.

"Sorry doesn't cut it, Evelyn," he growled, his tone dripping with disdain. "You're pathetic."

The memory shifted again, and now Evelyn was cradling her pregnant belly, sitting on the bathroom floor. She whispered softly to her unborn child, her voice trembling but filled with love. "It's going to be okay," she said, stroking her stomach gently. "I promise, I'll keep you safe."

But the tears streaming down her face betrayed her words. She was scared—terrified, even—and yet, she carried on. Her love for her child seemed to give her the strength to endure, to survive another day in this house that felt more like a prison.

At work, she transformed into a beacon of light—a nurse who cared deeply for her patients, who always had a kind word or a reassuring touch. No one would have guessed the pain she carried, the battles she fought in silence. She wore her professionalism like a shield, her compassion like a second skin. But beneath it all, she was a woman slowly breaking under the weight of her reality.

As I watched these memories unfold, my heart ached for her. Evelyn was more than just a nurse, more than just a victim of her circumstances. She was a survivor, a woman who gave everything she had to others, even when she had nothing left for herself. And yet, there was a part of her that still hoped, still believed in the goodness of the world, even as it seemed to crumble around her.

My stomach turned as I watched this side of her life unfold. The strong, confident woman I knew was reduced to a trembling figure. But even in her pain, there was something in her eyes—a mix of love and resignation. She loved him, despite everything. And she wouldn't leave.

The next thing I saw was Evelyn in a hospital room, her arms cradling a newborn baby girl, her smile so genuine it brought tears to my eyes. The baby's cries filled the room, and Dr. Pike stood by her side, his expression unreadable. Evelyn's joy radiated from her as she whispered softly to her child, her love pouring out in every gesture. For a moment, it was as though nothing else mattered—her world revolved around the tiny life in her arms.

But as I watched, I couldn't shake the weight of what I'd seen before. Evelyn's love for her husband, her resilience, her joy for her child—it was all so painfully intertwined with the darkness she endured.

But then I was pulled into a memory I wish I could unsee.

Evelyn was moving about, trying to quiet her crying newborn. She rocked the baby gently, her voice low and soothing as she hummed a lullaby. Her eyes were heavy with exhaustion, but her love for her child shone brightly even in the darkest of moments.

Dr. Pike burst through the front door; his face contorted in frustration. He tossed his bag onto a chair with a loud thud and sniffed the air. "What the hell is that smell?" he barked, his tone sharp enough to make Evelyn flinch.

"It's dinner," she said softly, trying to keep her voice steady. "I made your favorite."

He strode over to the table, picked up a forkful of food, and tasted it. His face twisted into a scowl, and he spat it out onto the plate. "It's too salty! Can't you do anything right?" he shouted, slamming the plate down so hard it rattled.

Evelyn didn't respond. She turned her focus back to the baby, her hands trembling as she tried to soothe her child. The infant's cries filled the room, a stark contrast to the suffocating tension between Evelyn and Dr. Pike.

"Can't you shut that thing up?" he snapped, his voice cutting through the baby's wails.

"She's just a baby, Thomas," Evelyn said, her voice wavering but still calm. "She's hungry. I'll feed her in a moment."

Dr. Pike's face darkened. He stepped closer to Evelyn, his movements slow but deliberate, like a predator cornering its prey. "Don't talk back to me," he growled, his voice low and menacing.

Evelyn turned away from him, cradling the baby as she moved toward the crib in the corner. She gently placed the infant down, her hands lingering for a moment on the tiny body, as if drawing strength from her child. As she straightened up and turned back toward the kitchen, Dr.

Pike's hand came out of nowhere, striking her hard across the face.

The force of the blow sent Evelyn stumbling backward. Her head hit the countertop with a sickening thud, and she crumpled to the floor. The room fell eerily silent, save for the faint cries of the baby and the ragged breathing of Dr. Pike.

Panic set in as Dr. Pike knelt beside Evelyn's still body. "Evelyn?" he said, his voice shaking. He pressed his fingers to her neck, searching for a pulse. Finding none, he began chest compressions, his hands trembling as he counted aloud.

"Come on, damn it!" he yelled, his voice a mixture of desperation and fury. But it was no use. Evelyn's lifeless body lay there, unmoving, her face pale and serene.

Dr. Pike sat back on his heels, his breathing heavy as the reality of what he had done sank in. He ran his hands through his hair, muttering to himself, his eyes darting around the room as if searching for a solution.

Minutes later, he moved with cold precision. He wrapped Evelyn's body in a sheet and loaded it into the trunk of his car. The baby, now calm and quiet, was placed in the car seat. Dr. Pike drove to the hospital, his knuckles white as he gripped the steering wheel, his mind racing.

He entered through the back door, the one rarely used by staff, and made his way to the boiler room. The air was thick and warm; the loud machinery filled the space. At the farthest, darkest corner of the room, he placed Evelyn's body into a large, unused box, carefully closing it as if sealing away his guilt.

Dr. Pike stood there for a moment, staring at the box. His jaw clenched, his mind already crafting a narrative to cover his tracks. He reached into his pocket and pulled out a lighter. With one flick, a small flame danced in the dim light. He crouched near a pile of old, discarded hospital supplies, setting them ablaze. The fire caught quickly, the flames licking at the walls and spreading with alarming speed.

He stepped back, watching as the fire consumed the room. The heat was intense, the smoke thick and acrid, but he didn't move until the alarms began blaring. He slipped out unnoticed, blending into the chaos as staff rushed to evacuate the building.

It wasn't a patient who started the fire; it was Dr. Pike.

As the fire raged, something extraordinary happened. Evelyn's ghostly form emerged from the smoke, translucent yet unmistakable. She moved with purpose, her steps sure and steady as she entered the burning wards. Patients cried out in fear, and staff scrambled to help, but Evelyn—ethereal and calm—guided them, her voice steady and soothing.

Evelyn's ghostly form was a vision of calm amidst the chaos, her ethereal illuminated by the orange glow of the raging fire. The thick smoke curled around her translucent body, but she didn't falter. Her movements were purposeful, almost as if the flames themselves gave way to her. Where others stumbled in panic, she stepped with grace, her focus unshaken.

The first patient she came across was an elderly man trapped in his bed. The flames licked at the curtains near his window, and the room was quickly filling with smoke. He coughed violently, his frail body trembling with fear. Evelyn appeared beside him, her presence both startling and calming. Her hand rested lightly on his shoulder; he seemed to feel her reassurance.

"It's going to be okay," she whispered, her voice a soothing melody that cut through the chaos. She leaned over and unlocked the brakes on his bed, pushing it with ease toward the door. The smoke parted as she moved as if the elements themselves respected her determination. She guided the bed into the hallway, where panicked staff and patients were scrambling to escape. A nurse turned and spotted the bed, his eyes widening in confusion.

"Who—?" the nurse started but stopped himself, too overwhelmed to question how the bed had gotten there.

In the next room, she found a young woman cradling her newborn. The mother's face was streaked with tears, her cries of desperation muffled by the suffocating smoke. The baby wailed, its tiny lungs struggling to take in air. Evelyn knelt beside the woman, her ghostly presence a comforting balm.

"Follow me," she urged as she signaled the woman to follow her. Evelyn reached out, her hands steady, and took the baby from the mother's trembling arms. As if compelled by some force, the mother rose to her feet and followed Evelyn out of the room. The baby stopped crying; its tiny body relaxed in Evelyn's arms as she carried it to safety.

Evelyn didn't stop, didn't pause to rest. She moved through the corridors, guiding those who couldn't find their way and calming those who were overcome with fear. In one room, she found a young boy frozen in panic. The fire had cut off his path, and he was pressed against the wall, his eyes wide with terror. Evelyn approached him, her presence like a soft breeze cutting through the stifling heat.

"You're stronger than this," Evelyn said, her voice gentle but firm.

Evelyn followed close behind, ensuring he made it to safety before disappearing once more into the chaos.

The flames grew fiercer, and the air was thick with smoke, but Evelyn pressed on. In one room, she found a man who had fallen from his wheelchair. He was coughing violently, unable to lift himself up. Evelyn knelt beside him, her ghostly hands slipping beneath his arms as she helped him back into his chair.

Room by room, patient by patient, Evelyn worked tirelessly. Her ghostly figure moved like a beacon of hope, her presence seen and undeniably felt. The chaos around her seemed to bend to her will, the flames retreating just enough to give her the space she needed to work. The alarms blared, and the staff scrambled, but Evelyn remained a steady force, guiding, protecting, and saving.

And then, as the last of the patients were pulled to safety, Evelyn stood at the center of the hallway, her ghostly form surrounded by smoke and ash. She looked back at the flames, her expression serene. She had done all she could, given everything she had. Slowly, her figure began to fade, her light dimming until she was no more.

Even in death, Evelyn fulfilled her sacred oath as a nurse—a promise to heal, protect, and serve, no matter the cost. In the face of unimaginable chaos, she stood as a silent guardian, her compassion and dedication transcending the boundaries of life and death. Her spirit didn't waver; instead, it burned brighter, illuminating the path for those who needed her most. Evelyn proved that the essence of a true nurse is not confined to a beating heart but lives on in the actions taken and the lives touched—even beyond the grave.

I gasped as I was yanked back into the present, my legs trembling beneath me, barely able to hold me up. Evelyn's ghost stood before me; her translucent figure was calm yet weighed down with an unspeakable sadness. My heart pounded in my chest as my eyes drifted to the corner of the room. That's when I saw it—a burnt box, charred and forgotten, sitting like a grim relic against the far wall.

My breath hitched. I knew what it was. It had to be.

I turned to Evelyn, her figure flickering faintly, and whispered, "Is this...?" My words trailed off, the weight of realization pressing against me like a vice. Her gaze didn't shift, but there was something in her eyes—a plea, a quiet kind of pain that twisted my stomach.

I took a step toward the box, my feet feeling heavier with each movement, like I was walking through water. The room was suffocatingly silent, the air thick with anticipation. Just as I reached out to touch the box, a shadow shifted in the corner of my vision.

"What are you doing here?"

The voice made me freeze. It was sharp, panicked, and unmistakably familiar. I turned slowly, and there he was— Dr. Pike. His face was pale, his features twisted in a way I'd never seen before. This wasn't the calm, composed man I'd encountered in the halls. This was someone unraveling, a man on the edge of losing everything.

"What do you think you're doing in here?" he demanded, his voice shaking but forceful.

I swallowed hard, my pulse roaring in my ears. "I know," I said, my voice cracking but resolute. "I know everything. About Evelyn. About what you did."

His face contorted, his eyes darting to the burnt box and then back to me. "You don't know anything," he snapped, but his voice wavered, betraying the truth. "You don't understand. It's not what you think."

My anger surged, breaking through my fear. "I understand perfectly," I said, my voice rising. "You killed her, didn't you? You hid her body in here, started the fire to cover it up! You've been lying to everyone all these years!"

Dr. Pike staggered back as if I'd struck him, clutching his head with both hands. "No... no, it wasn't supposed to be like this!" His voice cracked, and he started pacing erratically. "I didn't mean to—she... she wouldn't stop!" His words dissolved into incoherent muttering, his hands pulling at his hair, his steps frantic and uneven.

My chest tightened as I watched him unravel. I took a cautious step back, glancing toward the doorway, but he caught my movement.

"You don't get it!" he shouted, his voice sharp and ragged. His hand dove into his coat, and my blood turned to ice as he pulled out a gun.

"Dr. Pike, no!" I raised my hands instinctively, my heart pounding like a drum. "You don't have to do this."

His hand shook, and the barrel of the gun pointed directly at me. His eyes were wild, darting between me and the burnt box. "She's everywhere," he said, his voice breaking into a sob. "I can't... I can't escape her. She's always here."

I tried to steady my voice, though tears were streaming down my face. "Dr. Pike, listen to me. You're not going to fix this by doing something you can't take back. Evelyn wouldn't want this."

His expression twisted, a strange mix of anguish and fury. "You don't know what she would want!" he screamed. "You don't know anything!"

The room seemed to tilt as he raised the gun higher, his finger trembling on the trigger. "Please!" I begged, my voice cracking. "Think about what you're doing!"

But he was lost, too far gone. His finger pulled back, and the sound of the gunshot shattered the air.

I stumbled backward, a searing pain exploding in my chest. I fell to the ground, the impact knocking the wind out of me. My ears rang, the world around me blurring into a haze. I could hear my heartbeat slowing, each thud louder and further apart.

I blinked, struggling to stay conscious. Through the haze, I saw her—Evelyn. She stood over me, her expression heartbroken, her translucent hand reaching out as if to comfort me. "Evelyn..." I whispered, though the word barely escaped my lips.

She knelt beside me, her form glowing faintly. I felt her presence warm and calm despite the chaos around us. I tried to speak, to say something, but the darkness was closing in. The last thing I saw before my vision faded was Evelyn's sorrowful gaze, her lips moving silently.

Then, all I could hear was silence.

CHAPTER TWELVE: LOST LIVES AND LIVES SAVED

I woke up to the sound of laughter, soft and distant, like the echo of a memory long buried. As my vision adjusted, I realized I wasn't in the hospital anymore. Instead, I stood in a cozy living room with sunlight filtering through sheer curtains, casting soft patterns on the walls.

I felt an ache deep in my chest, but I didn't know why. The scene before me was familiar, yet I couldn't place it. Then I saw her. A younger version of myself—no older than three—sitting cross-legged on the floor with a tattered stuffed bear in my arms. My tiny hands clutched it tightly as if it were my only lifeline.

Confusion swirled in my mind. *What is this? Why am I here? Am I dreaming?* I took a step forward, but my feet felt heavy, as if the air itself resisted my movements.

The door to the living room creaked open, and Melissa, my stepmom walked in, she looked so young, vibrant, and full of life. Her hair framed her face like a gentle halo, and her smile was warm enough to melt the hardest of hearts.

"Hi there," she said, crouching down to my three-year-old self's level. Her voice was soft and kind, a sound that wrapped itself around me like a comforting blanket. "You must be Lila."

I watched as my younger self tightened her grip on the bear, hesitant but curious. Melissa didn't push. She sat patiently, waiting for the little girl to decide whether to trust her. She reached into her bag and pulled out a book, holding it out like an offering.

"I brought something for you," she said. "It's my favorite story when I was your age."

Little Lila's curiosity got the better of her, and she inched closer. I could feel the weight of that moment, the beginning of a bond that would change my life. Melissa's voice filled the room as she read the story aloud, her words painting pictures in the air.

I stood there, watching the scene unfold, my chest tightening with emotion. This was the first time I met her, the woman who would become my mother in every way that mattered. But why was I seeing this? Why now? *Am I dead?*

"She's going to be your new mom," a voice said behind me. I turned to see my dad standing in the doorway, looking uncertain and hopeful.

My mom had been gone for as long as I could remember. Her absence was a hole I didn't know how to fill. But this woman—this stranger who smiled like sunshine—was offering me something I didn't know I needed.

I looked back at her. She watched me with so much warmth and love that it made my chest ache. She never forces herself on me. She never asked me to call her mom. I have called her by her first name ever since. But that didn't make her any less than a mother. It was never a problem. She would often tell me how she loved that I treated her like my best friend.

She reached out and gently brushed a crumb from my cheek.

I watched as the younger version of me slowly crawled toward her, curiosity replacing fear. She opened the book, her voice carrying the words in a way that made the room feel less empty. For the first time in as long as I could remember, the silence was gone, replaced by the sound of her voice and the comfort it brought.

I stood there, an invisible observer in this memory, tears prickling at my eyes. This was the moment I met the woman who would change my life, the woman who would become the mother I didn't even know I needed.

The memory shifted, and suddenly, I was in the kitchen as a teenager, flour-dusting the counters as Melissa and I attempted to bake cookies. She laughed as she smeared a streak of dough across my cheek, and I retaliated by flicking flour at her. The air was filled with laughter, the kind that made your ribs ache and your cheeks hurt.

"You're going to burn this house down if you don't mix that batter properly," she teased, her eyes twinkling with mischief.

"Only if you don't set it on fire first," I shot back, grinning.

The warmth of the moment was almost too much to bear. I wanted to reach out and hold onto it, to freeze this memory and stay in it forever. But the scene faded again, and I was thrust into a different time.

I found myself in a memory I wasn't ready to see. At first, I thought I was dreaming, but the weight of it, the vividness—it was all too real. I was sitting in the passenger seat of my own car, staring at myself as I climbed into the driver's seat. I was wearing the scrubs, Melissa, my stepmom, had given me as a gift.

The dashboard glowed faintly in the dim morning light: *August 12, 2024.* My stomach dropped. That was the day Melissa died.

I watched myself muttering under my breath, rushing like I always did. "Shit, I'm late," I heard myself say as I tossed my Stanley mug into the cupholder and my purse onto the passenger seat. I cringed at the sight of my frantic movements, completely oblivious to the chain of events about to unfold.

I started the car in the memory, weaving through traffic like I was racing the clock. When the main road clogged up, I veered onto the back streets. It was a shortcut I'd taken dozens of times before.

I watched as I blew past a stop sign without so much as a glance. My chest tightened as my eyes darted to the rearview mirror in the memory. I saw a car that swerved and hit a concrete barrier. It was Melissa's car.

She had tried to stop. I could see it so clearly, the way her car swerved to avoid mine. Then came the sound. The screeching of tires, the deafening crash of metal on metal. I froze, tears streaming down my face as I sat helpless, forced to watch it all unfold.

The past me kept driving, unaware of what I'd caused. All I noticed was a faint honk and a noise I dismissed as distant. My breath hitched as I watched myself park at the hospital, grab my bag, and walk inside. I wanted to scream at myself, to shake myself out of my ignorance, but I couldn't. All I could do was follow.

Inside the hospital, I watched myself go about my routine—clocking in, tying my hair back, putting on a brave face for another shift. Then the announcement came.

"Code trauma, ETA two minutes."

I followed myself into the trauma bay, and my heart shattered as the paramedics wheeled in the stretcher. I didn't need to look. I already knew who it was. But still, I couldn't stop myself from looking. Melissa.

She was pale, her body limp, blood staining the edges of the gurney. The trauma team worked around her with precision, but I already knew how this would end. The memory of that day had haunted me for so long, but this time, I was seeing it with a clarity that made it unbearable.

The heart monitor flatlined. The attending physician's voice cut through the silence, clear and final.

"Time of death: 0930 a.m."

I sank to the floor, my legs too weak to hold me. My sobs echoed in the memory, raw and unrelenting. How could I have not known? How could I have been the cause of this?

Before I could spiral any further, the memory shifted again. I was standing in the same hospital hallway where Melissa had first appeared to me as a ghost. But this time, she wasn't asking if she was dead. This time, she was looking at me with the same warmth she always had, her voice calm and steady.

"It wasn't your fault, Lila," she said, stepping closer.

I shook my head, the guilt choking me. "It was, Melissa. I didn't stop. I didn't even notice you were there. I—I caused the accident."

She placed her hands gently on my shoulders, grounding me. "No, sweetheart. It's not your fault. It was meant to happen"

"But if I'd just—"

"It doesn't matter now," Melissa said firmly, her eyes locking onto mine with a warmth that somehow steadied the storm inside me. "What matters is what you do moving forward. You have a gift, Lila. It's time you embrace it."

I shook my head, the guilt still a knot in my chest. "But—if I had just stopped at that sign—"

"Then maybe something worse would have happened," she interrupted, her tone gentle but unwavering. "You didn't see it, but a mother and her child were on the corner that day, about to cross the street. They were on their way to school. When they saw my car crash, they stopped. If they hadn't, another car coming through that intersection who was a drunk driver would've hit them."

Her words settled heavily in the air, making my breath hitch. "So, you're saying—"

I was thrust back into the memory—the same one that had been haunting me. I was in my car, gripping the wheel tightly as I rushed through the back streets, the familiar sense of urgency and panic washing over me like a cold wave.

I could see it so clearly now, as though the memory itself wanted to punish me. My car cruised through the intersection, and in the distance, I spotted her—my stepmom. She was coming through the same crossing in her car. The moment my car entered her view, she swerved hard, trying to avoid me. The screeching of her tires, the sound of metal crashing, the echo of a horn—all of it hit me like a blow.

But that wasn't all. From the corner of my eye, I saw them: a mother and her young son standing at the edge of the sidewalk, just a few steps away from crossing the street. They had been about to step off the curb, the little boy clutching his mother's hand as they waited for a clear path.

When they saw my stepmom's car crash, they froze, instinctively running toward her wrecked car instead.

And then I saw it—the truck. Barreling down the road, swerving erratically. The driver, clearly drunk, ran the same stop sign I had ignored just moments before. Within a split second, it roared through the intersection, narrowly missing the mother and her son by inches.

My heart pounded as I stood frozen, watching the memory play out before me. My stepmom's crash—the chaos it caused—had stopped that mother and her child from crossing. That drunk driver would've hit them directly if they had been just a few steps farther into the street.

I glanced at the fading image of her car, the way it had shielded that mother and her son, the lives it had unknowingly saved. And then I thought about her—my stepmom. The way she always gave so much of herself, even in her final moments. Her love, care, and belief in me lingered like the faint warmth of a fire long after the flames had gone out.

"You see?" she said, standing beside me as I got pulled back in that moment where she was standing behind me. "It wasn't your fault, Lila. You couldn't have known what would happen. But what you think of as a mistake—it saved lives that day."

"I'm saying things happen for reasons we can't always understand," she said, her voice softening. "It doesn't erase the pain or the loss, but it also doesn't mean it's all on you. Sometimes what feels like a tragedy in one moment becomes something that saves someone else in another."

Tears slipped down my cheeks as her words sunk in, the knot in my chest slowly loosening. "I don't know if I can believe that" I admitted.

"You don't have to believe it all at once," she replied, her smile faint but filled with love. "But you must start letting go, Lila. Not everything is your fault, no matter how much it feels that way. What you do with your gift now—that's what matters."

She smiled, her expression full of love and understanding. "You've always been able to see things others can't. To help those who linger, those with unfinished business. Use it, Lila. Don't let fear hold you back."

Tears blurred my vision as I tried to process her words. "I'm sorry, Melissa," I whispered. "For everything."

"It doesn't matter now," she interrupted softly. "What matters is what you do with what you've been given. That mother and her son are alive because of what happened. The future has a way of balancing itself, Lila. You must let go of this guilt."

Her words wrapped around me like a blanket, steadying my trembling hands. The memory began to fade, but not before the mother's grateful, tear-streaked face burned itself into my mind.

Her smile didn't waver. "There's nothing to be sorry for. I'm proud of you, Lila. Always."

And just like that, she was gone.

The glow she left wasn't something I could touch or see, but it was there, constant and undeniable. It was in the lives she'd touched, the love she'd given, and the strength she'd passed on to me. It was the light I now carried within me, ready to shine for those who needed it most.

#

I slowly regained consciousness, the cold floor of the old wing pressing against my back. My chest burned with pain, each shallow breath a struggle. The dim lights above me flickered, casting shifting shadows across the room. My vision was hazy, but I could make out a figure leaning over me—Luis.

Luis must have followed me into the old wing, though I didn't realize it at the time. Later, I would wonder why—did he have a hunch, a gut feeling, or was it just pure luck? But in that moment, as I stood frozen, staring at Dr. Pike's trembling hands holding a gun pointed at me, Luis was quietly lurking in the shadows, observing the unfolding chaos.

He saw everything. The way Dr. Pike's face twisted in desperation and rage, the way his finger hovered dangerously over the trigger. Luis knew this was no idle threat. Slowly, he backed out of the room, pulling his phone from his pocket, and with shaking hands, dialed 911. He whispered into the phone, trying to keep his voice calm while explaining the situation: a man with a gun, the old wing, and a hostage.

Then, the sound.

The deafening bang of the gunshot shattered the silence like glass, and Luis ran back in without thinking. His heart was pounding as he skidded into the room, finding me crumpled on the floor, blood pooling around me. I could feel his hands on me instantly, applying pressure to my chest, trying to stop the bleeding.

"Stay with me, Lila," he said, his voice cracking but firm. "Don't you dare close your eyes. Help is coming."

Dr. Pike stood there, still holding the gun, his expression unhinged and unreadable—part denial, part horror. He was muttering to himself, pacing the room, running his free hand through his hair. Luis, still holding pressure on my wound, looked up at him.

"Doc," Luis said carefully, his voice low and steady despite the terror in his eyes. "You don't want to do this. Just... put the gun down. Let's end this without any more blood."

Dr. Pike's muttering turned into a loud laugh, sending chills through the room. "She knows too much. She's ruined everything!" he spat, his words sharp and venomous. "You don't understand what I've done. What I had to do!"

Luis didn't flinch. He glanced down at me, still conscious but fading fast, and adjusted his grip on my chest wound to keep me stable. Blood seeped through his fingers, but he kept the pressure constant.

"I don't need to understand, Doc," he said firmly. "What I do know is that this isn't the way. You're a doctor—you save lives, remember? Put the gun down. Let the police handle it."

The sound of distant sirens filled the air, growing louder. Dr. Pike froze, his eyes darting to the doorway. Panic replaced the anger on his face.

"No... no, no, no. They can't take me. They'll never understand!" he shouted, his voice cracking.

The sirens grew deafeningly close, and the flashing red and blue lights danced through the cracked windows of the old wing. Luis didn't dare move, but he whispered down to me.

"They're here, Lila. Just hang on a little longer. You're going to be okay."

"Dr. Pike, drop the weapon!" an officer barked, his gun pointed on the man. Luis glanced over his shoulder, his body shielding mine as he tried to de-escalate the situation.

"Doctor, please," Luis said, his voice calm but urgent. "It's over. Just put it down. She needs help."

For a moment, it seemed as if Dr. Pike wouldn't comply, his grip tightening on the gun. But then his shoulders sagged, and the fight drained out of him. The gun clattered to the floor as officers rushed in to apprehend him. His cries echoed through the hallway, a broken man unraveling as they led him away.

"Help is on the way," an officer assured Luis as he continued to apply pressure to my wound.

I remember looking up at Luis through blurred vision, his face etched with determination and fear, and the last thing I heard before slipping into unconsciousness was his steady voice whispering, "You've got this, Lila. Just stay with me."

My vision swam again, and I felt the edges of my consciousness slipping. But just before the darkness could claim me, I saw her—Evelyn. She stood near the edge of the room, her form illuminated by a faint, ethereal glow. Her expression was serene, her hands clasped in front of her as she gazed at me.

I tried to speak, to call out to her, but no words came. Evelyn gave me a soft smile, one filled with gratitude and peace. Slowly, her form began to fade, the light around her growing brighter until it was almost blinding.

And then, like a flame gently snuffed out, she was gone.

Luis's voice pulled me back. "Stay awake, Lila. We're taking you to the ER."

Tears welled in my eyes, not from the pain but from the overwhelming sense of peace that washed over me. Evelyn was gone—truly gone. Not trapped in the old wing, not lingering in the shadows. She had found her rest, her eternal glow dissipating into the light.

For the first time, I felt a quiet sense of closure, knowing she was finally free. As the team arrived and began their work, I clung to that thought, the glow that Evelyn and Melissa left behind illuminating something in me I hadn't realized I needed. Peace. I never saw them again.

CHAPTER THIRTEEN: BACK TO THE LIVING

I woke up to the sound of chatter. My eyelids felt heavier than my body, and when I managed to open them, I was greeted by the off-white ceiling of a hospital room. The familiar beeping of the heart monitor kept time with my throbbing chest. I tilted my head slightly, and there they were—Luis, Rowan, and Maggie—standing at the foot of my bed, engaged in a lively conversation about something trivial, like whether pineapple belonged on pizza.

"She's awake!" Luis exclaimed, stepping closer with a broad grin. "Told you she's indestructible."

Rowan leaned over; her expression soft. "Don't scare her with your loudmouth, Luis. Lila, how're you feeling?"

I tried to speak, but my throat was dry, so I croaked instead. "Like I got hit by a truck."

"Well, you kind of did—metaphorically speaking," Maggie said, her voice laced with concern. "But you're here, and that's what matters."

Luis shoved a small bag of chocolates onto my tray table. "These are for when you're sick of hospital food. Don't tell anyone I smuggled them in."

I smiled faintly, though the weight of recent events pressed heavily on me. I asked about Dr. Pike, about the police, about what had happened after I lost consciousness, but the fatigue was overwhelming.

"What happened to... Dr. Pike?" I asked.

Luis exchanged a glance with Rowan before he spoke. "Don't worry about him, Lila. He's where he belongs now. The police took him in."

"But—" My voice cracked, but I pressed on. "What happens now? What did they find?"

Luis took a deep breath, his tone cautious but firm. "They're charging him with murder, Lila. Turns out, he killed his wife—Evelyn. Told everyone she ran off with another man, but it wasn't true. Her body... it was in a box, Lila. Right there, close to where you were shot."

I stared at him, my mind reeling, as images from the old wing came flooding back. "A box?" I whispered.

Rowan nodded, her expression somber. "Yeah. From what they're saying, he put her body there after... after it happened. And when he tried to cover it up, he started the fire."

Luis said, his voice low. "It wasn't a patient smoking near oxygen, like everyone thought. It was him. He started it to cover his tracks."

"Rest for now," he said, patting my hand. "We'll fill you in later."

The story blew up, shaking the town to its core. News Headline

Nurse's Remains Found Fifty Years Later in the Old Wing of Nightfall Pines Regional Hospital. Suspect Identified as Husband and Renowned Head Doctor, Dr. Thomas Pike.

They stayed a little while longer, their chatter both comforting and surreal. It felt like any other shift break at the nurse's station; except I was in bed. Eventually, they left, promising to check in on me later.

The first few days off were a blur of recovery—painkillers, physical therapy, and an endless stream of concerned text messages. But now that the physical pain had dulled, the mental strain began to creep in.

I couldn't stop replaying the scene in the old wing. Evelyn's glowing form, her sorrowful smile, the haunting revelation of who she was and what she'd endured. And then... her absence. She was truly gone now, leaving behind a legacy I was only beginning to piece together.

As I sat in the driver's seat of my car, I stared at my phone for a long time before dialing a number I hadn't called in months.

My dad picked up after the third ring. "Lila?" His voice was thick with sleep, but the warmth was unmistakable.

"Hi, Dad," I said, my voice catching slightly. "Did I wake you?"

"Doesn't matter," he replied, his tone softening. "What's going on? Everything okay?"

I hesitated, unsure how to begin. "Yeah, I mean... kind of. I just... I've been thinking a lot about Melissa lately."

There was a pause on the other end, long enough for me to hear him shifting in bed. "Melissa? What about her?"

"I don't know," I admitted. "It's just... I guess I never told you how much she meant to me. She wasn't just my stepmom. She was... she was like my real mom."

His breath hitched, and for a moment, I thought he might start crying. "She loved you, Lila. Like her own. You know that, right?"

I nodded, even though he couldn't see me. "I think I'm only starting to understand how much."

"She always worried about you," he said after a moment. "Even when you were grown. She'd always say, 'Lila's going to do great things, but I just want to make sure she knows she's enough.'"

Those words hit me harder than I expected, and tears blurred my vision. "I... I miss her, Dad."

"I miss her too," he said, his voice cracking slightly. "Every single day."

There was a long silence between us, but it wasn't uncomfortable. It felt like we were both sharing the same space, even from miles apart.

"Dad," I said finally, "she said she's proud of me, do you think that's true?"

"Proud?" he repeated, his voice suddenly firm. "Lila, she was always proud of you. She used to tell me that every chance she got. She'd say, 'That girl has a heart bigger than anything I've ever known.' And she was right."

I wiped my tears, a small smile forming on my lips. "Thanks, Dad. I needed that."

"You're a lot like her, you know," he added. "More than you realize."

That comment stuck with me long after I hung up. As I lay in bed that night, I thought about Melissa—not just the love she gave me but the strength and resilience she carried, even though I was just her stepdaughter. To her, I was her daughter.

She didn't have to choose me, but she did. And that choice shaped everything I am.

Melissa wasn't just someone who left a glow behind— she was my glow.

#

When I returned to work three weeks later, the hospital felt both familiar and strange. The ER was as chaotic as ever, with patients spilling into the hallways and the phone ringing off the hook. Luis greeted me with open arms.

"Welcome back, superstar," he said, his grin as wide as ever. "Don't expect any special treatment. You're still stuck with the graveyard shifts."

"I wouldn't have it any other way," I replied, my voice steadier than I expected.

I sat at the nurse's station, fiddling with a pen, still trying to wrap my head around everything that had happened. The memories of Evelyn, the old wing, and Dr. Pike were almost too vivid. My chest ached—not just from the wound but from the weight of it all.

Rowan plopped into the chair beside me, setting down her coffee cup with a thud. "So, how's it feels being a local hero?" she asked with a smirk.

I rolled my eyes. "Hero? Hardly. I'm just glad the truth came out."

Rowan leaned in, lowering her voice. "Honestly? I always knew there was something off about Dr. Pike."

Luis, who had just walked up with a stack of charts, stopped in his tracks. "Rowan," he said, his tone warning, "don't start."

"What?" Rowan said, throwing up her hands. "I'm just saying. The guy gave me the creeps. Always so... controlled. Like he was hiding something."

Luis sighed, shaking his head as he took the seat across from us. "You know we shouldn't be talking about this. It's over. He's in jail. End of story."

"It's not over," Rowan shot back. "Not for Lila, at least."

They both looked at me, and I shrugged. "She's right. It's not over for me. Not yet."

Luis rubbed the back of his neck, looking uncomfortable. "I get that, Lila. But digging into this isn't going to help. You need to focus on healing."

Rowan snorted. "Healing? How do you heal from finding out your boss was a murderer? And not just that— he almost killed you!"

"Rowan," Luis snapped, his voice sharp.

"No, let her talk," I said, surprising myself. "She's not wrong. I can't just brush this off like it's nothing."

Rowan gave me a grateful nod. "Exactly. Look, Luis, I'm not trying to stir the pot, but we all knew there was something... dark about him. He was too perfect. Too polished. And don't even get me started on how he'd lose it over the smallest things."

Luis sighed again, leaning back in his chair. "Okay, fine. I'll admit it. The guy had a temper. But I never thought he was capable of... that."

"None of us did," I said quietly. "But the signs were there. We just didn't see them."

Rowan leaned forward, resting her elbows on the desk. "You know, Lila, you're braver than any of us. You faced him."

"I didn't uncover anything, though," I said, shaking my head. "I just... happened to be there."

Luis reached out, placing a hand on mine. "You did more than that. If you didn't go there, no one would have checked the area, and they wouldn't have found Evelyn's body."

The mention of Evelyn sent a shiver down my spine. I could still hear her hum, still see her smile. "I just wish I could've done more," I said softly.

Rowan sat back, crossing her arms. "You did enough. More than enough."

We sat in silence for a while, the weight of the conversation settling over us. Finally, Luis broke the tension with a chuckle. "You know, if Rowan's ever in charge, we're all doomed."

"Hey!" Rowan protested, laughing. "I'd make a great charge nurse."

Luis rolled his eyes. "Sure. You'd be too busy gossiping to actually do any work."

Their banter was a welcome distraction, but my mind kept drifting back to Dr. Pike and Evelyn. I couldn't shake the feeling that there was more to the story—something I was still missing.

As the night went on, I found myself wandering the halls, my thoughts racing. I passed by the old wing, now sealed off with caution tape. I stopped for a moment, staring at the darkened corridor.

Rowan's words echoed in my mind: *I always knew there was something off about him.*

Maybe she was right. Maybe we all knew, deep down, that Dr. Pike wasn't the man he pretended to be. But we looked the other way. We told ourselves it wasn't our place to question him.

I thought about Evelyn—how she'd stayed behind to help, even in death. She'd been the light in the darkness, the one who refused to let fear stop her from doing what was right.

I wasn't sure I could ever live up to her example, but I knew I had to try.

Everything seemed the same as I walked through the halls, yet I felt different. The events of that night lingered like a shadow, but I also felt a strange sense of closure.

As I settled back into my routine at the hospital, something gnawed at the edge of my mind—a loose thread I couldn't ignore. Evelyn. A motherly figure who had saved me countless times and guided me in ways no one else could. But amidst all the chaos, the memories, and the haunting revelations, one question stood out like a flashing warning sign:

What happened to Evelyn's daughter?

If Evelyn's unresolved issue was finding justice for her death, then had she ever looked for her child? Did she know where she was? The thought sent a chill down my spine. I had seen Evelyn's love for her baby in those memories, her quiet resilience and fierce determination to protect her child even in the face of unimaginable abuse. But now, it felt like an empty chapter, an unfinished story.

CHAPTER FOURTEEN: THE TIES THAT BIND US

I found myself retracing steps I didn't even know I'd taken, pouring over everything I could remember. The photos in the old wing, the echoes of her presence, the way she carried herself as both a nurse and a mother. She'd given so much, even after death. But for all her strength, did she find peace in knowing her daughter was safe?

The question haunted me through my shifts, lingering like a shadow in the back of my mind. I tried to focus on the patients, on the bustling chaos of the ER, but Evelyn's face— her smile, her glow—was etched into my thoughts.

I turned to Luis, unable to keep my thoughts to myself any longer.

"Luis," I began, my voice hesitant, "do you know anything about Dr. Pike's daughter?"

Luis glanced up from his charting, arching a brow. "His daughter? Why do you ask?"

I shrugged, trying to appear casual, though my pulse quickened. "I don't know. He just seems... complicated. I was curious if he has a family."

Luis leaned back in his chair, tapping his pen against the edge of the desk as he thought. "From what I've heard, they're estranged. Haven't seen each other since she was, I think, 18? Something like that. But don't quote me on it. I've only caught bits and pieces over the years."

"Estranged?" I echoed, feeling a pang in my chest. "Do you know why?"

Luis shook his head, a look of mild pity crossing his face. "Not really. The guy's a bit of a mystery. You'd think for a doctor who's been here so long, we'd know more about him, but he keeps to himself. Some of the older staff might remember more about him, though. Why the sudden interest?"

I hesitated, biting my lip as I searched for an answer that wouldn't sound suspicious. "I don't know. I guess I just...

I've seen a lot of complicated families come through here. Makes you think about what people are dealing with behind the scenes."

Luis nodded, his gaze softening. "Yeah, everyone's carrying something. And from what I've heard whatever happened with his daughter, it runs deep. He killed her mother."

Everything seemed normal, but my mind wasn't. It was restless, caught in a web of unanswered questions. Dr. Pike was behind bars, but his story wasn't over. Not for me.

I didn't know why, but something pulled me toward his office. I stopped in front of the door; the police tape stretched across it like a warning sign. My breath hitched as I stared at the yellow barrier, debating whether to step inside. The rational part of me knew I shouldn't be here, but curiosity—and something deeper, something unnamable— drove me forward. Before I could second-guess myself, I slipped through the tape and into the office.

The air was stale, heavy with dust and disuse. It smelled faintly of old books and something metallic. The room was cluttered with papers, medical journals, and empty coffee cups scattered across the desk. Yet, despite the chaos, it felt frozen in time, like the aftermath of a storm.

My eyes fell on a framed photo sitting on the desk, partially obscured by a stack of documents. I picked it up, brushing off a thin layer of dust. It was a photo of Dr. Pike and his daughter. Dr. Pike stood stiffly beside a girl with a bright smile and wide eyes. She couldn't have been older than nine or ten. There was something eerily familiar about her face, but I couldn't place it. My heart quickened as I studied her features, searching for the connection that felt just out of reach.

Setting the photo down, I moved to the desk drawers, my hands trembling slightly. I wasn't sure what I was looking for, but I had a gut feeling there was more to this story. The first few drawers held nothing but the usual office supplies—pens, notepads, paper clips—but when I opened the bottom drawer, my breath caught.

Inside was a stack of papers tied together with string. Nestled among them was a folded letter, its edges worn and frayed as though it had been read countless times. I hesitated, my pulse thundering in my ears, before unfolding it.

The handwriting was small and neat, but the emotion in the words was impossible to miss.

Dad, I'm tired of you controlling every part of my life. Please don't come looking for me. Every time I asked about Mom, you shut me down or got angry. You told me mom went with another man, but I know that was a lie! I deserve to know the truth, but you never told me anything real. If you can't be honest, then don't bother finding me. I'm done.

At the bottom, the signature stopped me in my tracks: *Melissa.*

I sat frozen in the chair, the letter trembling in my hands. The signature, *Melissa*, glared back at me like a beacon, tying together pieces of a puzzle I hadn't even known I was solving.

Shaking, I placed the letter back into the drawer, my fingers brushing against something else beneath the stack of papers. I pulled out a small, worn envelope. Inside were more photographs—dozens of them, spanning years. My breath hitched as I shuffled through them, each one revealing more of the story.

One photo stopped me in my tracks. It was a portrait of a young girl, maybe sixteen years old, her dark hair pulled into a neat ponytail. She was sitting in what looked like a high school gymnasium, wearing a cheerleader uniform, her smile wide and carefree. My chest tightened as I stared at the image. Beneath it, scrawled in delicate handwriting, were the words: *Melissa, age 16.*

It was her. My stepmom.

My heart pounded as the realization started to sink in— Melissa, my stepmom, had been Dr. Pike and Evelyn's daughter. I swallowed hard, trying to make sense of it all. How had I not seen it before?

I lingered on one photo. It was a picture of a tiny newborn cradled in Evelyn's arms. Evelyn looked radiant, her face glowing with joy as she gazed down at the baby swaddled in a soft pink blanket. Her hands were steady, protective, and full of love. My heart clenched as I realized the newborn was Melissa. Beneath the photo, in faded ink, were the words: *Melissa, just a few hours old.*

The image of Evelyn as a young mother, full of hope and love for her child, struck me deeply. This was before everything fell apart before secrets and pain overshadowed their lives. Evelyn's expression was so tender, so full of promise, that it was almost unbearable to look at. I could feel the weight of all the years that had passed since this moment, the tragedy that had followed, and the echoes of a life that never had the chance to bloom the way it should have.

The letter in the drawer and the pictures scattered across the desk painted a picture of a family fractured by secrets and lies. Melissa's yearning to know the truth about her mother, Dr. Pike's controlling grip on her life, and Evelyn's tragic end—it all connected. And somehow, through fate or chance, I had been pulled into their story.

I set the photo down carefully, my mind racing. I couldn't stop staring at Melissa's face, trying to reconcile the vibrant young girl in the photos with the woman I'd known. The woman who had been my mother when I needed one most. The woman who had kept her pain hidden so well that even I, who loved her deeply, had never suspected the weight she carried.

Memories of Melissa flooded my mind. Her laugh, her warmth, the way she always had a kind word for everyone. But now, I couldn't help but wonder what she'd been hiding behind her smile. How many times had she thought of Evelyn? How many times had she questioned her father's version of events? How many nights had she cried herself to sleep, wondering where her mother was?

I wiped at my eyes, trying to clear the tears that wouldn't stop falling. I had come here looking for answers, but what I found was something far more personal. This wasn't just Evelyn's story—it was Melissa's, too. And somehow, it was mine now.

I looked at the desk one last time before standing. The weight of what I'd uncovered felt almost unbearable, but I knew I couldn't turn away from it. These were the truths Evelyn and Melissa had carried with them that shaped their lives and deaths. And now, they were mine to hold.

As I stepped out of Dr. Pike's office, I whispered softly into the silence, "I'll make sure they remember you. Both of you."

The halls of the hospital felt different as I walked back to the main floor. Every step felt heavier like the knowledge I carried had changed the very air around me. But it also felt lighter, like I was one step closer to giving Evelyn and Melissa the peace they deserved.

Now I know why Evelyn is finally at peace. She's reunited with Melissa in the afterlife, a mother and daughter together again, free of the pain and suffering that haunted them. As I stood there, letting the weight of it all settle in my chest, I realized something profound—I was at peace, too. Knowing that Melissa, the woman who had been such a good mother to me despite never experiencing a mother figure growing up, was no longer alone gave me solace.

I imagined that Evelyn and Melissa had found each other, and in their reunion, I found a sense of closure I didn't even know I needed.

The glow they left behind wasn't just a memory—it was a reminder of the love that endures, even beyond death.

CHAPTER FIFTEEN: WHAT WAS LEFT BEHIND

Nightfall Pines became my home in ways I never imagined. Its walls, steeped in past whispers, taught me more about life and death than any textbook or mentor ever could. The once-daunting halls now carried the weight of familiar steps, each echoing a story. Every shift reminded me of my purpose—to care, to connect, and to understand. It was no longer just about the living but about honoring those who lingered, their lives echoing in ways most could not perceive.

I wasn't the same person who first stepped into this hospital. That Lila was unsure, burdened by questions she didn't have the courage to face. Now, I moved through my days with a sense of quiet resolve. I had accepted my gift, and in doing so, I had accepted myself. My role was no longer just about healing bodies—it was about mending hearts, soothing spirits, and helping those caught between to find peace.

For the living, I was their nurse, their confidant, the steady hand in moments of chaos. For the dead, I was something else entirely—a bridge, a keeper of their unspoken truths, their unfinished stories. Each soul I encountered left an indelible mark on me; a spark of their light added to my own. Evelyn, Melissa, and all the others— they weren't just memories. They were my teachers, my guides. Through them, I learned what it truly meant to hold space for someone, to carry their pain without letting it consume them.

The hospital became my sanctuary and my battlefield. Every day brought its challenges—the cries of newborns, the grief of goodbyes, the quiet resilience of those clinging to hope. I found joy in the small victories, like a patient's first smile after a long illness, and sorrow in the losses that came despite our best efforts. But even in the sorrow, there was beauty. Every life, no matter how brief, left behind a glow— a legacy of love, resilience, or longing that deserved to be remembered.

One evening, as I prepared for another long night, I stood in the dimly lit ER, watching over a patient who had finally drifted off to sleep. The stillness of the moment wrapped around me like a warm blanket, offering a rare moment of peace. But then, it came—the familiar chill that raised the hairs on the back of my neck. I paused, my breath hitching as the air seemed to shift around me.

I turned slowly, scanning the empty hallway behind me. At first, I saw nothing but shadows stretching across the floor. Then, I caught it in the corner of my eye—a faint, flickering glow, like the remnants of a candle struggling to stay lit. It moved slowly, almost hesitantly, as if waiting for me to notice.

"Lila..."

The voice was soft, barely above a whisper, but it carried the weight of a thousand echoes. My heart raced, not with fear but with a strange mix of anticipation and understanding. I had felt this before—the unmistakable presence of someone who wasn't ready to leave.

I turned fully toward the hallway, my eyes searching for the source. The glow seemed to retreat, drawing me toward the shadows. I hesitated, glancing back at my patient.

Taking a deep breath, I stepped into the hallway, my footsteps barely audible against the polished floor.

"Who's there?" I asked, my voice steady despite the unease creeping into my chest.

The light shifted, coalescing into the faint outline of a figure. It was too indistinct to make out features, but the presence was undeniable. It didn't move closer, didn't speak again, but the weight of its gaze—or what felt like a gaze—anchored me in place.

"I'm here," I said softly. "Tell me what you need."

The glow flickered, dimming until it vanished entirely. The hallway was silent again, but the air felt heavier, as if it had absorbed the presence of the soul that had just departed.

I stood there for a moment, letting the stillness settle over me. These encounters no longer frightened me.

As I returned to the ER, I felt a quiet resolve settle in my chest. This was my purpose, my calling. Nightfall Pines Regional Hospital had become more than just a hospital to me—it was a place of healing, of connection, of redemption. It was where the living found solace, and the dead found peace.

On my way out, I passed the hospital chapel. Its stained-glass windows glowed faintly, the light from the streetlamp outside casting fractured rainbows on the polished floors. I stopped for a moment, drawn by an unexplainable pull. Inside, the pews were empty, but the air carried that same charged stillness.

"Hello?" My voice echoed faintly.

Nothing.

I shook my head, laughing softly to myself. I was letting my imagination get the better of me. It had been a long shift.

But just as I turned to leave, I felt it—a cold breath on the back of my neck. My heart stopped. Slowly, I turned around. There, in the farthest corner of the chapel, was a shadow. It wasn't just a trick of the light—it moved, shifting slightly, as if watching me.

"Is there something you need?" I asked, my voice trembling.

The shadow didn't respond, but the faintest whisper reached my ears. It wasn't words—just a sound, low and sorrowful, like the wind carrying a distant cry.

I backed away, my pulse quickening, but something stopped me. For reasons I couldn't explain, I whispered, "I'll be here when you're ready."

And then, just like that, it was gone.

The chapel was empty again, the glow from the stained glass casting its soft hues across the silent room. I exhaled shakily and walked out into the night.

Not all spirits are ready to move on, and not all of them are easy to help. Some are angry, vengeful even, trapped in their pain and bitterness. They're the ones who linger the longest, caught in a loop of reliving their final moments or clinging to the grudges they carried in life.

I've seen them before—spirits pacing the same hallways, muttering the same words, over and over. There was one, a man, who sat in the waiting room night after night, staring at the door as if expecting someone who never came. Another, a woman, whose cries echoed through the stairwell, trapped in a memory of abandonment. They haunt not just the hospital, but themselves, unable to let go.

Some spirits aren't just lingering; they're thrashing against the chains of their unresolved pain, their anger sharp enough to cut through the air. They don't want help. They want vengeance. Their presence is heavier, darker, like the hospital itself trembles under the weight of their fury.

I remember one night when I felt it—a cold that wasn't just temperature, but a biting chill that clawed at my resolve. I followed the sensation to the ICU stairwell, where the lights flickered more than usual. At the bottom of the stairs, a shadowy figure appeared, pacing. It was a man who'd died unexpectedly during surgery, his whispered accusations filling the stairwell: *"They didn't try hard enough. They let me die."*

He wasn't ready to hear the truth. He didn't want comfort; he wanted someone to blame. He lunged at me, his shadowy form dissolving into the walls, but the anger lingered like a stain on the air. I couldn't help him—not yet. He wasn't ready to let go of his pain, and until he was, he'd remain, trapped in his own torment.

These spirits—the ones who are too far gone in their rage or grief—are the hardest to face. They don't seek closure; they seek retribution. Their glow is muted, almost snuffed out, replaced by something jagged and broken. They circle their old wounds, unwilling to move beyond them. And I've learned, painfully, that I can't rush their journey.

One was a woman I encountered in an area long abandoned and used only for storage. I was walking past when the sound of faint sobbing reached my ears. It was rhythmic, almost hypnotic, and I felt drawn to it. When I stepped inside, the air was thick with bitterness. She stood there, her form flickering, clutching an old hospital gown. Her child had died in that very room, and she blamed everyone—the doctors, the nurses, even the machines.

Her grief had curdled into anger, and her presence turned violent. She hurled objects at the walls, her screams so sharp they felt like they could slice through my skin. *"They promised to save her!"* she shouted. I tried to speak to her, to calm her, but she lunged at me, her form dissolving into a gust of icy wind that knocked me back. She wasn't ready. Her pain was too fresh, too consuming.

Another time, I felt an overwhelming sense of dread in the stairwell leading to the old wing. I'd heard stories of a man who fell down those stairs while fleeing security years ago, his anger at being caught fueling his final moments. When I reached the landing, he was there disjointed, like his spirit couldn't fully piece itself together. His rage was palpable. *"They stole my life!"* he hissed, the words reverberating through the empty stairwell.

He lashed out, his shadowy hand grazing my arm. For a moment, I felt his pain and saw flashes of his life—desperation, regret, and betrayal. But his anger was like a fortress, and he refused to listen no matter what I said. He paced the stairs endlessly, trapped in his own loop of blame and fury.

And then there was the older man in the ICU waiting room. His wife had died on the operating table, and he'd passed away just days later in that very room, his heart unable to withstand the grief. Now he lingered, his form translucent, sitting in the same chair where he'd spent his final hours. But instead of mourning, he was enraged. *"She wasn't supposed to go first!"* he shouted one night, slamming invisible fists into the wall.

His presence scared the living, his form casting eerie shadows that sent chills through anyone who passed by. He didn't want comfort or understanding; he wanted to haunt those he blamed. Even when I tried to speak to him, his voice would rise into a crescendo of accusations.

But I still whisper to them when I can:

"When you're ready, I'll be here. I'll help you find the light, the peace you deserve. I won't give up on you, even if you've given up on yourself."

Some nights, their shadows feel closer, their whispers sharper. And I wonder if they'll ever come to me or if they'll remain forever in that dark limbo. But I hold onto hope. Even in the deepest anger, I've seen glimmers of something more—a longing for freedom, for relief.

But I've learned that even the angriest spirits have a crack in their armor, a small opening where their true longing lies. It's not vengeance—it's understanding, validation, or closure. Until they're ready to face that, though, they remain here, looping through their anguish like a broken record.

I've stood in the presence of their fury, felt the chill of their despair. And though they may lash out, I remind myself of one truth: their glow is still there, buried deep beneath the shadows. It's just waiting for the right moment to break through.

I know I can't force them to heal or to move on, but I'll be here when they're ready. It's all I can do—offer them a presence, a voice that reminds them they're not forgotten, even in their rage or sorrow. Sometimes, that's enough. Sometimes, it isn't. But I'll wait because even the angriest spirits deserve a chance to find their glow.

#

The weeks turned into months, and I continued my work, weaving between the living and the departed. Each encounter left me with something new—a lesson, a reminder, a story. I often thought of Evelyn and Melissa. Knowing they had together now brought me peace, but their absence also left a void I wasn't sure could ever be filled. Still, their glow lingered, guiding me in ways I couldn't fully explain.

On the last day of the year, I stood at the entrance of the hospital, looking back at the building that had given me so much. The lights in the hallway flickered faintly, casting long shadows that seemed to move on their own. I smiled, feeling the presence of something—or someone—watching over me.

I turned to step into the crisp night air when a sound stopped me in my tracks—a familiar hum, delicate and haunting. It drifted down the hallway, soft and rhythmic, carrying with it a melody I had heard so many times before.

Evelyn's hum.

It sent a shiver down my spine, not of fear, but of something else entirely—a connection, a bond that time and death couldn't sever. I stood there, listening as it echoed softly, fading into the silence. My heart ached and swelled at the same time, a bittersweet reminder of the lives that had passed through these halls and the marks they had left behind.

At that moment, I understood. The glow they left wasn't in their lingering presence, nor in the whispers or the fleeting visions. It was in their stories—the love they gave, the struggles they endured, the connections they made. It was in the memories they entrusted to those who remained, and, in the lessons, they left behind. It was in me, in every breath I took, every patient I touched, and every soul I helped guide to peace. The stars above shone brightly as if the heavens themselves were glowing with the remnants of those who had come and gone.

Nightfall Pines has always had its whispers. It is a town that seems to fold stories into the air, where the living and the dead coexist, even if most never realize it. Over time, the tale of Evelyn—the ghostly nurse who saved countless lives during the fire—became one of those whispers. People spoke of her heroics with reverence, never knowing that I, of all people, had uncovered the truth.

But the truth didn't matter as much as the glow she left behind—the inspiration she became. She was the nurse who defied death to ensure life endured. A legend to them, a reality to me.

The town doesn't know this side of me. They don't see me speaking to shadows, comforting the restless, guiding those who are ready to cross over. To them, I'm just Lila, the nurse who stayed. They make up their own stories, whispering about the glowing nurse in the old wing or the mysterious hum that echoes through the halls at night.

In their eyes, Nightfall Pines is haunted—but they'll never know just how deeply.

One night, as I made my way through the empty, shadow-drenched halls of Nightfall Pines, the stillness was suffocating. The flicker of the fluorescent lights cast strange, wavering shapes that moved even when nothing else did. My steps echoed, each one louder than it should have been as if the very walls were listening.

And then, I heard it again.

A hum—low, haunting, and drawn out, like a song long forgotten. It crawled through the air, sending a shiver so sharp it felt like icy needles piercing my spine. It was a sound I knew too well, familiar and yet... wrong.

"Evelyn?" I whispered, my voice cracking against the silence.

The hum didn't stop. It grew closer, weaving around me like a phantom hand brushing against my neck. My heart pounded; each beat a deafening drum in my ears. I turned slowly, my eyes darting down the corridor, expecting— dreading—what I might see.

The shadows shifted unnaturally, pooling in corners and stretching across the walls. The air was heavy now, pressing against my chest as if daring me to breathe. The hum twisted, the tune warping into something darker, something sinister. It was no longer soothing. It was mocking. It was imitating Evelyn's hum.

And then I saw it.

A figure stood at the far end of the hallway, barely visible in the faint glow of a dying bulb. Not Evelyn. This presence was something else entirely. Tall, unnaturally gaunt, with hollow eyes that bore into me even from a distance. It stood motionless, the mocking hum spilling from its throat, its lips never moving.

I froze; my breath caught in my throat. The air grew colder, my skin prickling as if frost had begun to creep across the walls. The figure tilted its head, and for a moment, I thought I heard it whisper, just beneath the hum—a word, a name, or perhaps just my imagination playing tricks. But then it began to step forward, the hum growing louder, the shadows stretching toward me.

I turned and ran, my legs trembling with every step. The hum followed me, echoing through the corridors, rising to a maddening pitch. The sound abruptly stopped when I reached the nurse's station. Silence rushed in like a crashing wave, but the chill lingered.

I didn't look back. I couldn't.

Deep in my heart, I knew that *not every glow they leave behind brings warmth*. Some leave dark shadows that never truly fade.

As I stood there, frozen in the growing darkness, I knew something that didn't just want help had come through.

A chilling, deep, guttural voice slithered from the shadows, the syllables drawn out like a haunting melody, almost like singing, "*Liiiilaaa, Liiiilaaa, Liiiiilaaa....*"

It wanted me. And it's not going to leave me alone.

THE END

If you or someone you know is experiencing domestic violence, know that you are not alone and that there is help available.